FROM THE SIDELINES

FROM THE SIDELINES

RACHEL LABERGE

Paperback ISBN: 979-8-9891308-8-7

Editing by Kendra with Curious Minds Editing.

Cover design by Elen Bushe

Also by
Rachel LaBerge

THE PLAY CALLER SERIES
YOUR PLAY TO CALL
YOUR RULE TO BREAK
YOUR SECRET TO KEEP

THE Emerald Canopy Lodge
A LODGE AFFAIR
WHEN THE SNOW SETTLES

STANDALONES
THE ONE BED RULE
a love letter to those who left me behind

PLAYLIST

4ever | The Veronicas
Adore You | Maisie Peters
You Are In Love | Taylor Swift
Heaven In Hiding | Halsey
Make Me Feel | Janelle Monae
Comfortable | H.E.R.
We're In Love | boygenius
Sugar in the Tank | Julien Baker, TORRES
Proof | Paramore
Now or Never Now | Metric
The Louvre | Lorde
Ruin The Friendship | Demi Lovato
Man I Need | Olivia Dean
Little of Your Love | Haim
Scared of Loving You | Selena Gomez
Wood | Taylor Swift

LETTER FROM THE AUTHOR
Rachel LaBerge

I'm going to talk a little bit about the book in a second... this will include content warnings. If this isn't your vibe, feel free to turn the page. Quick.

Get out of here.

Don't get mad at me!

Last chance...

Okay, first, I want to start by saying this is a work of fiction. The way Blair finds a spot on the Cosmos roster is something that could actually happen—I didn't make it up. Now, has this ever happened? No. But, feel free to suspend reality for the next few hundred pages and enjoy.

FROM THE SIDELINES is an open-door romance with explicit content and language. There is mention of body dysmorphia and abandonment of a parent. As always with my books, there will be mental health representation and on-page discussion.

Please take care of yourself.

xoxo- Rach

For anyone who was told "that's not for you," and did it anyway.
This one's for you.

And to everyone who's ever told a woman to "name five players", may your
day be as dull as your personality.

One

Blair

"IF YOU WANT TO do another Nickelback themed spin class, you'll need to get at least six people to commit. Beforehand." I lean forward on my desk, elbows resting on the paper schedule I'm drafting for the next month. "Do you have six people?" I ask the question even though I probably already know the answer.

"I have three," Bella says, eyes wide and hopeful.

"Well, when you have three more, we'll put one on the schedule." My smile is sincere as I make some final notes based on our meeting and wait to see if she's going to push back. When she doesn't, a wave of relief hits me—as someone who despises rejection, it's hard to also reject others.

In my defense, we tried the class twice, and each time it was Bella and one other person. It cost me money to simply have the class on the schedule and, unfortunately, I'm not in the position to hand out cash. Having six people attend would cover the cost of the instructor and that's the best I can do.

Bella nods. "You got it." She smiles, her blonde ponytail bouncing as she leaves my office.

Ember and Ashes is my dream come true. A gym focused on women feeling safe and confident. We offer a variety of classes and make sure there's a strong emphasis on functional fitness. While the business is woman forward, everyone is welcome—as long as you're not a creep or an asshole.

I open my laptop to finish the weekly financials. My stomach rolls, the same way it does when I look at the books, even though we've been open for three years. While we've slowly grown our memberships, we've always toed the line of making money. After paying me, which is always last, we typically have a little leftover to fix a piece of equipment, or save for when we need it, and when you run a small business, you always need it.

We're killing it in vibes and attitude, even if we're not in the bank account. I'm hoping this is the year I can really grow our revenue—take us to the next level. Which is why I can't let Bella do another Nickelback spin class, no matter how bad I know she wants to.

My phone buzzes with a message:

Tyson

still on for tonight?

The smile that hits my lips immediately makes me feel lighter. I text him back.

Me

absolutely

considering we haven't been able to get together since your move

meet you there

Tyson Bishop. We've been friends since college—we met informally when he saved me from an icy demise on campus and then formally at a student athlete mixer our sophomore year. But since he ended up in the NFL and on a team across the country, we haven't seen a lot of each other.

Tyson was recently traded to the Upstate Cosmos—New York's newest football team. He's one of the best offensive tackles in the league and I'd be lying if I wasn't thrilled he wound up in the same state as me. Getting traded has to suck, but I'm sure the contract of more than one hundred million dollars makes the sting more manageable.

When the finances are finished, I take my final lap around the gym. It's a habit I've gotten into: look at how much money we've made or lost, then pause to take a moment and see what I've built. It's surprisingly busy for a Tuesday, with many of the machines in use, and people filing out of spin classes or waiting for yoga.

This doesn't suck.

I go to the front desk and take a seat just as Tiffany—one of my favorite people and our Embers and Ashes office manager—helps a new member get signed up. This feeling is better than hot coffee on a chilly morning, which is really saying something considering I view coffee as basically sacred.

I'm looking out through the floor to ceiling windows to the busy street. When it's bustling with people, it's fun to see patrons stop and peer in the window, or pause when they see our signage.

"I didn't know this was an Athlala gym," the new member says, while signing her paperwork. The excitement bubbling around her voice warms my chest and also makes me want to give her an aggressive high five.

Embers and Ashes is an Athlala sponsored company. College soccer didn't bring me a career as a professional athlete like it did for Tyson, but it did bring me Athlala—an organization focused on gender equity in sports.

Without their support, I don't think I would've been able to get this place off the ground. I won a grant and was able to pair it with years of saving every extra dollar to jump all the way in on being a small business owner.

Life changing. And I've loved every minute of it. No matter how stressful.

There's no other situation where I'm sitting at the front desk of my own gym, with things I'm passionate about, watching people meander by on a picturesque street in Ashbury, right outside New York City.

The imposter syndrome typically rages but right now, there's a little voice that says: *it's called a glow up, babe.*

A WHISTLE COMES THROUGH my FaceTime, catching me off guard as I try to get dressed.

"I think you forgot you aren't wearing pants," Maggie says, pretending to fan herself.

"Ugh, sorry!" After I grab the jacket I was looking for, I make sure my thong and bare ass aren't facing the camera–my phone propped on the mirror so I can use both hands.

"Don't apologize but do feel to drop the deets on that glute routine because damn," she jokes, and it brings a twinge of heat to my cheeks. It's mostly missing her and the way we make each other laugh—plus maybe the smallest sliver of embarrassment. Since she's a world away, chasing bad ass tennis player dreams, we do a lot of random video calls like this.

Once I put on my favorite pair of skinny jeans and a leather jacket, I step in front of the mirror, bringing my phone with me. I'm checking myself out when Mags chimes in again.

"Quit touching your shoulders. The jacket looks good. You look hot."

Rubbing my upper arms, I try to push the doubt back, the one my truest friend can locate even when she's thousands of miles away. I've always been self-conscious of my muscles—the way my arms look in a tank top, the way my thighs have rubbed together my entire life.

I'm working on it—in therapy, in the mirrors I walk by and catch my reflection, and with the clothes I choose to wear.

You look strong.

This color is working for you.

Oh, hello triceps.

Why is being kind to yourself so fucking hard?

I shake out my hair—my signature, almost awkward, mid-length brunette waves— and reply, "Why are you looking at me like that?" I can feel Mags' side eye before I confirm it on the screen.

She crosses her arms, sitting back. "Oh, it's nothing. Just watching you nervously jitter about for your date."

This again.

"It's not a date. I haven't seen him in almost two years. Can say, pretty confidently, we're not dating."

"You know what I mean," she jokes.

I let out a slow breath and grin at my best friend. There's no use arguing with her. Considering Tyson and I have never even kissed, or had a drunken hook up back in college, I know we're just friends. We've just always been close. He's always made me feel comfortable, like a close friend does.

My alarm vibrates, telling me my time is up and it's time to go.

"Gotta go." I grab my crossbody bag, putting it on. "Love you to the moon."

"Love you to Saturn," Mags says, blowing me a kiss before the screen goes blank.

THE BRISK OCTOBER AIR licks my exposed skin. The sun is long gone and we're in the type of fall where it's still warm during the day but you need a jacket at night—hence the black leather jacket.

I can't remember the last time I went out to dinner. I limit myself to takeout once a week, considering I'm a decent cook and can save tons of money by using my kitchen. I swing the door open, *The Wild Sage* emblazoned on the host stand, and start to scan the room for Tyson.

He must've been watching the door because as my eyes find the corner of the room, there he is–eyes on me. Tall. Dark. A beard I've never seen him in person with. While his fingers rub the strap on his watch, a grin takes over his lips, and it's like a punch to the gut.

The air practically squeaks out of my lungs and I immediately start to cough. The hostess looks at me, those beautiful sympathetic eyes, as I cover my mouth and try to get it together. Why is coughing in public one of the most embarrassing things a person can do?

And because Tyson simply couldn't wait, he's in front of me in seconds. I barter with my body, promising one more annoyingly loud cough, before

I cover my mouth and refuse it anymore. I'd rather quietly choke than cough again.

"Blair, you okay?"

Holding my breath, trying to force the coughing fit to stop, I keep a hand on my chest as I say, "Yes. Just choked on my own spit."

Why the fuck did I say that?

Tyson laughs like he always does. He always tells me I'm his funny friend. Not sure if he means it or he's being nice.

No matter what, I take it. Because as I follow him to our table, I'm willing the blushing to leave my cheeks.

Two

Tyson

Maybe you don't have feelings for her anymore? my brain suggests, forcibly. But, I see her walk by the window, the wind rushing through her wavy dark hair. She struts in, her legs strong and muscular, and I can't stop staring at them. The way they lead into her perfect curves.

She's trying not to cough–one of her least favorite things to do in public.

I open my arms for her. "Blair, come here." She presses herself to me and I hug her for all the times I've wished we were in the same place during the last few years. This is the longest we've gone without seeing each other and she's just as stunning as she's always been.

She looks at me with eyes that shine like if sunlight were to hit a jar of honey. They're so gorgeous it's hard to explain to someone who hasn't witnessed them in person.

Blair lightly taps a hand to the side of my face. "The beard."

"You hate it?" My brows furrow.

"I love it," she gushes, a smile pulling at the corner of her lips.

Fuck. Just like that, I'm under her spell. But she's always been the thing I couldn't have. My feelings are still alive and practically thriving. Feelings that have no business taking up residence the way they have. Girls like Blair don't end up with the guy like me–the one who fits so perfectly in the friend zone.

Reluctantly, I end the hug. "Sit. I got us a bottle of rosé." I pull out her chair and gesture for her to take it.

"You don't even like pink wine." She grabs the napkin and puts it on her lap.

"I mean, it's not my favorite. But I know you love it." I try to play it off, like even if I didn't like it, I'd still order her a bottle and pretend to sip it.

Sitting across from her, I take her in. She's wearing a tight cream top, making her golden skin stand out, and a jacket I've seen her wear for years. As always, she looks effortlessly beautiful.

"I can't believe we're finally in the same state," Blair exclaims, leaning forward, her hands on the table. "You're here!"

I push my hands through my hair. "I know. It's been wild. Everything happened so fast. My agent gave me a heads up about ninety seconds before the old team called to tell me their version. Then the new team was trying to get ahold of me for logistics and delivering playbooks and, fuck. It was a lot."

"I can't even imagine." She shakes her head. "Where are you staying?" she asks, lightly pivoting, picking up the menu and looking at the starters—her favorite place to order from.

"I'm in the city. Found somewhere that was available a few days after the trade."

I don't like thinking back to it. The day I learned that no matter how good you are, how much you wish to stay with an organization, all teams are about making money. My previous team struggled the entire time I'd been there… always finishing close to the bottom. In eight seasons, I played in two playoff games—each ending in a pretty horrible loss.

Honestly, the end result never mattered much to me; I loved my coaches, the training staff, my teammates, the fans. So, when my agent called to tell me about the trade, just a few minutes before it went public, it fucking stung. Bad. Given that the Cosmos have won a Super Bowl already, and have a stacked roster, I thought it would hurt less, but it surprisingly didn't.

Part of me was excited to be in the same state as one of my college friends. Blair offered to help me move, figure things out, but I told her I had it under control. I didn't, but I couldn't let her see me like that. Things got dark for a while… dark in a way I hadn't felt in years. But it also helped with clarity. What I want to do. Who might be next to me when I do it.

"Can't wait to see it. Finally, a place to crash when I want to go to the city," she giggles as our server fills her wine glass.

"Any time," I say, and her eyes stay on mine as she peers over her menu. We hold for a second longer than what seems friendly, but I can't help it. Being here, in her orbit, fuck. I've missed this.

The server's voice interrupts us. "Anything you'd like to start with?"

Glancing down at the menu, I take a breath, knowing Blair is waiting for me. This is one of our things—ordering food for the table and seeing if we missed anything the other couldn't live without. That's how well we know each other.

"We're going to do some sharing. You can bring these as they're ready, split what's easy, if you can. We'll do the burrata with the pears and crostini, fried pickles, the smoked pineapple dole whip wings, a side of the blackened green beans, the cobb salad, and the PB&J burger."

Blair grins, her head tilting with each item I said.

"Anything else?" I ask her, tilting my head to match hers.

She hands the server our menu. "No. Sounds absolutely perfect."

When it's just the two of us, I lift my glass of rosé and we clink our glasses. "Nailed it," I say, right before I take a sip of the chilled wine.

Blair follows suit, taking a drink, but then lets out a tiny laugh. One I haven't heard in person for far too long. One that has always made my stomach flip.

WE'RE ON OUR SECOND bottle of wine and the plates have been cleared. Blair's cheeks are slightly pink, matching some of the flushing on her chest, the way she gets whenever she drinks wine.

Just like the first bottle, the conversation was easy. After we've covered everything from work to family, and football, it's time to get to the question I've been dying to ask.

"How's it going with Melanie?" I do my best to make my voice level and smooth, immediately chasing my question with wine.

Blair sighs. "It's not. We broke up." She shrugs her shoulders and I immediately scan her face for the hurt. "Don't look at me like that. It's not that deep. We're still friends, or pretend we *will* be, but it wasn't a good fit."

"Why didn't you say anything?" I look for a glimpse of her holding back.

"You had your own shit to deal with. You didn't need me piling on about my most recent failed relationship."

There she is. The woman who has tried to handle things her entire life without being a burden. The first time we met, it was winter and she was carrying too many bags, like she'd just been grocery shopping. Even though everything was a complete ice rink, she still tried to do the whole *'I'd rather almost die and do this in one trip'* thing. I offered her help, more than once, and she declined. When she fell and almost hit her head on the sidewalk, she reluctantly gave me her hand and let me assist.

Sometimes, she still needs to trip and figure it out before leaning on anyone else. She's tough as fuck even when she doesn't have to be.

"You don't ever owe me details or anything like that, but you don't ever have to deal with that shit alone. Breakups suck."

Setting her wine down, she replies, "I know. You're right. But honestly, it wasn't this big, sad thing. We just weren't compatible. She couldn't handle that I was bi and I don't see that changing any time soon, so..." She tucks her hair behind her ears. "What about you? Dating anyone?"

"Me? Nah. It's hard when you're gone like I am. I went on a few dates before I got traded, but nothing serious." I'm desperate to change the topic from my lack of dating or relationships so I pivot. "But, how have we not talked about how you were on my new team's football field before me?"

"Stop. It was a PR thing." She shakes her head, fighting a smile and rolling her eyes.

Athlala and the Cosmos were collaborating on a Women In Sports camp. They had some of their members, like Blair, help run it. The goal was to let the young girls try different sports—see if there's any they'd like to pursue.

"I love how you're acting like you didn't make a thirty-yard field goal on a legit NFL field. I'll never forget seeing that video and showing it to my teammates."

"It took me, like, twelve tries—that you didn't see. You know that Joey and Jay taught me how to kick a field goal when I was a kid. It's just something I can do. Not that good of a party trick... unless you're at a football game."

Blair loves to play down her accomplishments. I feel like she knows it was fucking cool but she's afraid to really lean into it.

"Whatever you say. Glad to see you're still in shape." I wink, joking with her, because she's one of the most committed and disciplined people I know.

She keeps shaking her head, taking a drink of wine, and my chest warms when I catch her grinning. It's like muscle memory—the way my heart stumbles. All this time, and she still feels like the weighted moment before a whistle blows: full of hope, full of something I can't name without ruining it.

<h1 style="text-align:center">Three</h1>

<h1 style="text-align:center">Blair</h1>

Fuck. Why does this man look this good?

He's always been thick and muscular, needing size to play his position. But now it's like he grew into it? I'm not sure how to explain it. He's always been attractive, but now he's making me practically drool with his new facial hair, and some sort of pullover sweater. It's almost a perfect match of his eyes—that nearly impossible shade of blue—the kind only found in the places you dream of, where the water never ends.

Maybe it's the wine? Or the borderline food coma?

Get it together.

"This is for you," Tyson offers as he sets a giftbag on the table.

"For what?"

"I missed your thirtieth birthday last month. You don't think I was going to let that slide, right?"

No. Tyson is one of the most thoughtful people I've ever encountered. No matter what, he's always found ways to celebrate my birthday, even if we weren't together.

He side-eyes me, those classic blues almost stopping me in my tracks. Pulling the bag closer, I reach in and pull out the first thing, an envelope with a field pass.

"Hope you can find someone to take your shifts at the gym. Tickets for Sunday's home game. Pre-game access, all the fun stuff." His smile is contagious as I pull out an Upstate Cosmos jersey—Bishop #67 on the back.

I hold it up to me and let out a laugh that might be a little loud for public. Fortunately, I look around and see most people have moved to the bar and a lot of the tables are empty.

"This is very fucking cool. I'm so proud of you!" I scoot my chair back, stand, and meet Tyson with my arms looped around his neck. His arms pull me closer, resting on my lower back. He sways back and forth while letting out his own laugh—it shakes us both.

"You didn't even get to the best part of the gift," Tyson says in my hair.

I sit, kicking my feet, and put my hands in the bag, pulling out a bag of coffee beans. Bringing the bag to my nose, I take in the deepest breath, trying to smell the notes and uniqueness of the beans. The aromatics hit me—my favorite smell in the world.

Coffee is one of the few things I don't budget or pay attention to when it comes to a price tag. I'm meticulous about keeping my equipment taken care of and absolutely love trying coffee beans from other roasters.

"You fiend," Tyson teases, shaking his head at me. "There's three bags. One for each away game I've had this season. Went on a mission to find you the best coffee from each spot."

"Ty. That's so sweet." He grins at the nickname, the one he's pretended to hate, but doesn't seem to mind when I use it. "Thank you for thinking of me."

He sucks in a breath, like he's going to say something. Instead, he takes a drink of water and follows it with a standard, "You're welcome."

Tyson always seems to remember the little details and puts other people first. Exhibit A: the second bottle of wine we're working on when I know he doesn't drink much during the season, and if he does, it's typically an IPA. But here's this burly man, drinking pink wine, without a care in the world.

He pours the rest of the bottle into our two glasses and one thought keeps running in my brain.

How is this man single?

"Woah, guess it's time for us to go," I say, looking around at the chairs flipped on tables. It looks like most of the restaurant staff has left, leaving only the closers behind.

"Time flies," Ty adds, standing up and pulling his phone out. "I'll get us an Uber."

Smart, considering we each had a bottle of wine. And a glass of bourbon with dessert, as recommended by the server. Apparently, it was the perfect match for the Pecan Pralines, and let me tell you, he was 100% correct.

Ty leaves an extra $100 bill on the table, probably because we stayed for hours and no one made us feel rushed. Hell, maybe they did and we just didn't pick up on it? Wouldn't be the first time. We have this way of getting wrapped up in each other, no matter if we're talking sports, the gym, family drama, or some meme on the internet.

We're waiting for the Uber outside, seeing the closing time on the door and realizing we're past it by almost an hour. The air has the chill of winter on its edges and it's windier than before. I try to wrap my arms around me, but that's difficult when I'm holding a gift bag, plus this jacket is much more for novelty than function.

Like Ty can read my mind, he wraps me in a bear hug. He's big and warm, and I don't know what kind of fabric this pullover is, but fuck, it's soft. Rubbing my back, he tries to warm me up—shield me from the cold.

And I don't resist.

Too quick, it seems, the Uber shows up. Tyson confirms the license plate, opens my door and helps me in before walking to the other side and sliding in next to me.

"What about my car?" I finally realize that tomorrow—well, today, considering it's after midnight—I will have work to do and places to be.

Tyson's face is illuminated by his phone. He swipes around a few times and hands it back to me. "Schedule an Uber to your apartment. Address and everything is typed in, just need to know what time."

Again, thoughtful.

"You think of everything," I say while trying to decide what time I'll want to be up and ready to go get my car and start my day. Ooof. Tomorrow may suck a little. But I'd do it again, no questions asked, to spend time like this with one of my favorite people.

We're on our way to my place first; it's about twenty minutes from here, and I can't get my hands warm. I'd rather melt into the Earth than ask the Uber driver to turn the heat up or be a burden in any way, shape, or form. I rub them on my jeans and try to put them inside the sleeves of my jacket, but nothing helps.

"Here," Ty says while reaching for my hands, which feel like icicles, and sandwiching them between his own.

His hands are massive and ridiculously warm. "Your hands are like bear paws," I tease while leaning my head to his shoulder and letting our hands fall between us.

Ty laughs. "Lots of encounters with bears since we've last caught up?"

I smile into him at the joke and feel my stomach flip, like when you start the drop of a rollercoaster.

Because him and I, sitting like this, his hands in mine. It feels like something I'd like to do again.

But we're just friends. The words rattle in my ribcage, thinking about the first time he said them, all those years ago.

I'd been waiting for him outside the weight room, sitting on the concrete bench with my backpack at my feet, swinging my legs just to burn off nervous energy. I had a great practice at the soccer field and couldn't wait to tell Tyson all about it.

The doors swung open, and I heard his laugh before I saw him. He was talking with a couple of his teammates, helmet tucked under one arm, bag on his shoulder.

"I told you," he said, "Blair's waiting. I have to go."

My chest warmed at the sound of my name—at the fact that he'd told them about our plans. It's been a minute since anyone could make my stomach flip like this. Actually, it's been months.

After the athlete mixer, the basketball-playing junior I was dating decided to end things. It wasn't that serious between us, but seeing him with someone the following weekend stung like lemon in a cut.

And then there was Tyson. Present whenever I needed him. Wearing a smile I'd never get sick of. He invited me to the party where I saw my ex—he was trying to get me to do something fun—and he felt so bad he ended up leaving to get me ice cream.

Tonight was going to be pretty lowkey with nothing elaborate planned, just getting homework done for classes, and maybe watching whatever NBA game was on.

The sound of the guys chatting pulled me back to the present. I could see them if I peeked around the pillar in front of me. One of them pressed, "Oh, so sorry! Forgot that your girl's waiting for you, Bishop."

I froze where I sat, my whole body lighting up at that—your girl.

Then came the questions, quick and relentless—were we a thing, had we kissed yet, was he ever going to make a move?

I gripped the strap of my backpack, heart hammering, waiting for him to smile and say yes, waiting for him to claim me in front of everyone.

Instead, he shrugged, casual as ever. "Nah. We're just friends."

Just friends. Two little words that knocked every bit of air from my lungs. One of the first times I realized how much I wanted something more but it wasn't in the cards to have.

They all laughed and moved on, still talking about weekend plans, but I couldn't make myself move. My throat burned as I slipped out before he could spot me, and I immediately put my cell phone to my ear, like I was deep in conversation. I had to put on the mask, convince him, before he could see the way those words—the ones I wasn't supposed to hear—shattered something I didn't have the words for yet.

Every once in a while, when I think Tyson is doing something that would put us in a different category—other than friends—that conversation comes roaring back.

It's just the thing to sober me up in the back of the car, even though Tyson's hands are still holding mine.

Four

Tyson

"THIS IS A FUCKING joke." The words fall out of my mouth, catching Coach and my teammates off guard.

"Bishop, I wish it was. We have no kicker. Our starter, back up, and free agent signing from two weeks ago are all injured. Out for the long haul." He must see my face because I definitely saw our third string kicker working out this morning, prepping for the game. "Jones had a non-contact injury during prep today. Looks like it's his Achilles tendon."

Wow. This is some bad luck. I don't know of any team who has lost three kickers in four weeks.

"Now, I wish we could just go for two after each score, but this defense is the best in the league. They've not allowed a two-point conversion in almost a season and a half." Coach stands, looking around like he's trying to collect his thoughts.

"Is this time for one of my famous ideas? It's bonkers... but it's better than nothing." Zack Andersen, long-snapper, and the only man I know who owns a 50% pink wardrobe, addresses the team.

Tapping his foot, Coach replies, "At this point, I'm open to even what you've got, Andersen."

Zack stands, his floppy blonde hair bouncing, and he rubs his hands together. "Hear me out. Odds are, someone here knows how to kick a field goal, or might be athletic enough to give us some type of a shot."

When everyone keeps staring, Zack fills the silence. "Let's do a call out for anyone who thinks they could make a field goal and see what happens."

"And then what? Sign them for the game?" Tripp, our star wide receiver, asks. Zack shrugs and everyone looks at Coach. The fact that he hasn't said anything makes me think he's considering it. "Can we even do that?" Tripp presses.

Coach takes a long breath, looking up at the ceiling before huffing it out. "Technically, yes. But you're right, this is bonkers." Coach's eyes roll when he uses the same term from Zack. "We'd have to get the brass to approve it and have all the paperwork dotted and signed ninety minutes before the game starts. Plus, then you shell out the rookie minimum, which is about eight hundred thousand fucking dollars." He presses his forehead with his fingers.

"You want to go back-to-back, right? Today is a hell of a matchup. They're in our division, on our side, this could be a tie breaker. We're both undefeated." Zack shrugs like we're talking about getting pizza or wings for dinner.

Coach looks to his staff. He delegates tasks: someone to get the GM and bring him here, someone to loop in the entertainment and announcers, team doctors to draft up the minimal amount of paperwork necessary, and the equipment manager to get one of each jersey size ready for customization.

It's four hours before game time, so we're definitely within the ninety minute window. We need to keep going through our pregame prep, but before we're dismissed, Coach half jokes, "If you have a sibling, friend, retired athlete, anyone in the building who you think can make an extra point, call them. Don't promise them anything, but get them on the field for this weird stunt that Zack dreamt up."

"Coach, is there any rule that says it has to be a guy?"

He laughs, and over his shoulder says, "No. Can be whoever."

Immediately, I'm thinking of Blair. I just saw her do this, more than once, and even a bit further than an extra point, a few weeks ago. She's coming to the stadium early—just have to get her on the field.

I KEEP LOOKING TOWARDS the seats, waiting for Blair. It's when I see her in my jersey that I realize I wasn't prepared. This is the first time she's sat this close to the field, where I can see my number, knowing it's *my* name on *her* back. Fuck—I can't move. This puts me in the wrong spot during the practice drill and a football hits me right in the chest. The laughter roars from my teammates, maybe some early fans, and I watch Blair cover her mouth with a hand—one I'm sure she's laughing behind.

Jogging over, I high-five the hands of some fans on the way. She crouches, looking at me through the railing—the only thing separating the fans from the field.

"Man, thanks for the tickets. This is amazing!" Joey, Blair's older brother, reaches down, giving me a high five. He beams and takes in the field in front of him.

I've always liked Joey. He gives Blair enough shit but ultimately cares about her and does his best to keep her out of harm's way—just like a big brother should.

"Yes! I love this!" Blair cheers, her eyes glittering like gold from the October sun while she almost bounces out of her skin.

Watching any sort of sporting event with Blair is an experience, and I say that as a compliment. She immediately immerses herself in the rules, easily picking up on the plays and objectives, and seemingly finds someone to cheer on no matter what it is. She has this way of sparking a change in the energy—it's one of my favorite parts of her.

"I heard they're doing some kind of on-field field kicking before kick-off," I say, trying to sound casual. "Don't let the boys have all the fun." I wag my finger at her, half-teasing. "You'll hear the announcement—and any security guard can walk you down once it starts."

Joey scoffs. "Like she'd EVER." He rolls his eyes and Blair stands, swatting him lightly in the chest with the back of her hand.

"Watch me." Her grin is quick and sure, the kind that makes my pulse stutter. "That actually sounds fun. I'll find my way down there." She tosses her hair over her shoulder, already scanning the crowd like she's figuring out her route. Then her eyes find mine again. "Good luck, Ty."

Fucking butterflies. Pre-game. I'm such a cheeseball.

After making a few announcements, there's about twenty people who think they can make an extra point. The media team is playing it off as a way to win some swag; even they have no idea our special team coaches are looking for someone to potentially kick for the team.

They line up and start kicking. Everyone gets two tries to make a field goal, and then they'll move it back a few yards until there's only one left.

"This is my kind of vibe," Zack says, standing next to me, rubbing his hands together like this all part of his master plan.

"You love a little chaos, don't you?"

He gives me a side-eye that says 'Of course I do,' and we watch people try, and mostly fail, to get the ball through the uprights. Most people, those barely or not athletic at all, and typically male, always berate kickers for missing but it's something that takes significant skill. You have to get the distance and the height right, which isn't a general skill people—or even professional athletes—possess.

A man, no more than twenty years old, is the first to make it. After that, someone probably my age squeaks one in—he's just as surprised to see it make the uprights as we are.

Blair is next. She's wearing these baggy jeans paired with my jersey—my number on her is something to remember. Catalog. Take a mental picture of. When she gives me a tiny wave to the sideline before she lines herself up, it takes everything I have not to loudly cheer her on. I tip my chin in her direction, letting her know I see her.

Zack notices and asks, "Wait, you know her? She's drop dead gorgeous in that jersey, my guy." He acts like he's going to fall to his knees—dramatic and typical.

I flick my head towards him—too fast—and Zack lifts his hands and takes a step away from me.

"Woah, chill, Icy-Tyson. I'm taken." He holds up his silicone wedding ring, wiggling it with a proud smile.

Shaking my head, I reply "What did I tell you about that nickname?" At first, it was T, and then it was Iced T, and then it was Icy Tyson. Honestly, it's hard not to laugh with him; he's truly the kind of guy who has best friend energy, even if you've just met. Zack was the one who gravitated towards me during the early camps and practices after the trade... and I'd be lying if I said I wasn't thankful.

He winks at me just before looking towards the field, as Blair kicks it through the uprights. She's excited but I know she's kicked from this distance, and made it, thousands of times. The deadpan look Zack gives me has me laughing, shrugging my shoulders.

"Maybe it's the jersey?" I joke, knowing Blair has been doing this since she was a kid—the product of always trying to keep up with her older brothers, and sometimes even being *better* than them.

There are only three people total who make the first kick. When they back it up another five yards, Blair goes first and sails it through like there was never a question. The crowd feeds into the hype, standing up and cheering for her.

Fuck yeah, Blair.

When the guy closer to my age misses, it's just Blair and the fresh-looking twenty year old. The two of them smile and laugh while they move the ball back another five yards—the true distance of an extra point. A voice booms over the stadium, the crowd getting into it, and says that each of them gets two kicks.

The guy hits the uprights on his first kick: miss.

Blair makes it and the crowd erupts—the kind of cheers you can almost feel through the turf.

On his last try, the guy sails it left—miss.

Blair lines up, even though she doesn't have to, and kicks.

And she fucking nails it.

Five

Blair

"YOU CAN'T BE SERIOUS." I have to remember to close my mouth because I'm standing in front of the head coach, special teams coach, and general manager for the Upstate Cosmos. Tyson, Joey, and *the* Zack Andersen stand behind me, watching this unfold.

Because there's no way someone just asked if I was available to kick in an NFL game today. Like, in two hours? And that would mean I'd be on the Cosmos roster. With a rookie minimum paycheck.

"What are you looking for?" the head coach asks as my head swivels corner to corner.

"Cameras. Someone filming in the corner. There's no way this is real." I laugh and put my hands on my hips.

Dylan, the special teams coach, jumps in, "We could be saying the same thing. How in the hell are you just walking around able to kick like that?"

"Older brothers. A competitive household. Soccer in college. I own a gym. I don't know?" The logical reasons fall out of my mouth, but it's still a long string of ramblings and it's hard for me to catch my breath.

"Stop it. She played D1 soccer.. Plus, she's fucking strong," Tyson interjects and I shoot him a look that begs him to stop talking.

Nerves creep up and flush my skin. I feel the warmth spread across my cheeks and I'm sure my hands are sweaty and disgusting.

"Here's the deal. We're out of options for kickers. The owners have the cash and are willing to do something that's never been done before. This game is critical and if having a shot at an extra point puts us in the best position to win later in the season, we're willing to do it." His eyes are glued to mine. "If you want, we'd like to make you the first woman on an NFL roster."

My head lolls forward, mouth hanging open—I can feel the deep lines dig into my forehead, the way I look when I'm trying to figure something out. Turning behind me, I look at Tyson.

"There's no way you're serious. It's very much giving *'this is a prank and I'm the butt of the joke.'*" The words are quiet but we're in a tight space—everyone hears it.

Zack Andersen, Super Bowl champion, casually strolls forward and puts a hand on my shoulder. "Listen, I get it. No pranks here. But you know what? It could be a fucking blast." He laughs and shakes me like we've met a thousand times.

What in the world is happening?

Tyson's wearing this smirk, almost like he's daring me to say yes. Or he wants me to. His blue eyes are unforgettably close to the Cosmos blue of his warmup gear.

"Blair, come on. Like you're going to let the boys have all the fun?" He says the phrase that he uses when he's trying to get me to do something. He points his words in a way that makes me feel like I can do it, and also like he already *knows* that.

The first woman on an NFL roster? On a random Sunday?

I take in a deep breath, rolling my shoulders away from my ears, letting the muscles relax all the way to the tips of my fingers. Closing my eyes for just a second, I stretch my neck, and sigh out the anxious air from my lungs.

Taking a page from my therapist's book, I try to clear my mind. Breathe through the noise until it's a blank canvas. *Can I do this? Do I want to do this?* It's not necessarily something I see, but I hear the sound of the whistle, the swell of the crowd. I feel butterflies in my belly and a smile pulling at my lips.

"I'm in. What's next?"

THE COSMOS FACILITY HAS quite literally anything you'd want, including a place to create my game wear for today. Clearly I have almost zero insight besides what Tyson has shared, but this is like a very modern, accommodating sports compound. Fancy as fuck.

After I practiced kicking inside—into a net with some of the special teams staff— and the quickest physical of my life, I'm now standing on the sidelines in a full Upstate Cosmos uniform.

Blair Miller, #7, possible extra point kicker, at your service.

This can't be happening. I look at my jersey, pinching the inside of my arm to prove I'm actually awake.

I keep finding Joey in the stands because bothering Tyson isn't the move. This is his actual job and I'm over feeling like some PR stunt experience maybe gone ridiculously wrong. The butterflies in my belly flutter about and keep stealing the air from my lungs—it's kind of rude, to be honest. When I see Joey, he claps and gives me an enthusiastic thumbs up.

I wish I could just be around Tyson but I don't want to be more of a distraction than I already am. The buzz around the stadium is almost tangible—like you can reach out and grab it—which tells me people are on to something. Believe me, I'd wonder why the random ass woman from the pre-game shenanigans is now donned in complete Cosmos gear, too. Like, who gave this rando a helmet?

The players line up and I'm trying to figure out if I do this? Where do I go? Just as I'm about to panic, internally of course, Zack lightly pushes me in front of him. Since he's the long snapper, and a key part of a successful kick after a touchdown, he's sort of made me his problem. He stays close, almost like he's ready to answer any questions that might come my way.

I turn and give him a small nod, but in my head it's like a mountain of forehead kisses and perfect coffee color and the cool side of the pillow whenever you need it. Zack seems to be as sweet as I've heard. I know he's one of Tyson's favorite teammates. Honestly, it's kind of reassuring that I'm not bothering Tyson—he can do his job while others check in on me.

When the burly head coach comes and stands next to me, I forget how to breathe.

"I don't know you but I think we're going to get along just fine. You've got bigger balls than some of the guys on the team. And if that's harassment, I'm sorry, but I want you to know how impressed I am."

The comment is borderline but we give the pass to the self-aware coach making his point.

"You already won today. You said you'd try something that's never been done and I want you to know that, before any points are scored. You seem like someone who might need to hear that." His hand finds my shoulder, now covered with a shoulder pad, and the softness from him calms the anxiety zipping through my bones.

When Coach offers the tiniest of one-sided smiles and walks away, Zack, who feels like my personal cheerleader, leans forward and says, "You know you got this, right?"

***The Cosmos are hurting—I'd be yelling at the TV if I was watching this game at home. We're down by six in the fourth quarter and it feels like I've been here for days. Time seems like it's walking through the sludge that is nervousness and anxiety.

Today was the perfect time for the Cosmos to test the two-point conversion play calls after scoring a touchdown. Today was also the perfect time to learn that this is a significant gap for the team. They're 0 for 4 on two point conversions and weren't able to convert on two fake punts they tried on fourth down–lining up for a field goal with a decoy kicker, to try and get the first down instead.

During halftime, I stood in the doorway of the locker room until someone waved me in. It truly didn't feel like I should be allowed in there. After the quick message from Coach, which was simply a longer version of "Get your shit together," some of the special teams' staff took me back to the net, having me kick a few more times.

Now, we're on defense in the fourth quarter, trying to get a stop. I feel Tyson slide next to me.

"How do I get one of those?" He points to my jersey, sweat dripping down his face.

"I'm not sure if I'll even get to keep *this* one," I joke, even though the staff told me I could a hundred times, because that's how many times I asked.

He bumps his shoulder into mine, "So, I feel like you'll appreciate the heads up. If we can stop them here, we're going to try and score and have you kick the extra point. If you miss, it goes into OT, and if you make it, we'll win."

I can't lose the game.

"Everyone is buzzing about how cool you are. The guys especially. But, I know you want to go out and show them how fucking *strong* you are." His smile hits me like a punch to the gut—good thing I'm wearing full pads.

Then his voice lowers, just enough that it gets lost beneath the roar of the crowd. "Hey," he presses, like he's afraid I won't hear him. When I turn, he's closer than I expect—helmet off, eyes soft in a way I've never seen from him before. "No matter what happens... I'm proud of you."

It's quiet, like it's only for him and I, but it lands like I'm being tackled. My throat tightens instantly. All I can manage is a nod, because if I try to talk, it'll break something open. His lips tug up on one side, offering a smirk, before bumping his shoulder into mine.

Shaking my head, I let out a smile. We both stand without another word and keep moving our bodies while we watch the defense.

They stop the team. No additional points scored. Still down by six. There's only two minutes left when Tyson jogs out with the offense. Zack has found his way to me, still taking me under his wing. I'm fairly certain they had Tyson come and mentally prepare me that I might actually be going out.

I can't help the excitement running through me. It's like when you know penalty kicks are coming in soccer—win or lose.

This is just like a penalty kick but less stakes. I repeat that mantra over and over as I bounce between my feet, keeping my legs ready.

The Cosmos offense seems to come to life, everything clicking and whirring like the machine they've built and quite literally paid for. Lineman block while running backs find gaps to sprint forward, collecting first down after first down. It's a twenty-six yard touchdown pass to Tripp Owen which has the clock running out and the Cosmos tying the score.

Coach calls a timeout and everyone huddles together. Zack playfully taps my helmet as I pull it on, waiting for the thing I know is coming. Coach looks at me, mimicking taking a deep breath, and gives me a thumbs up.

Everyone looks at me and it's like the world is tilting and my legs don't know how to manage the incline–even though I work at a fucking spin studio.

I know it's the anxiety. The stress. The nerves. But before I can let it consume me, Tyson stands next to me and says, "Those fucks think this is going to overtime." He points to the opposing team captains, waiting near the fifty yard line to run out for the overtime coin toss. "They think we have no shot. Do with *that* what you will."

Blame it on my brothers, or just being a woman in this climate, but I'm ridiculously competitive. I want nothing more to make this extra point. Tyson knows it, too. I'm thankful for the extra fire, for the chance to prove someone wrong.

The sound of the stadium seeps into my bones, getting louder with each step I run out on the field. Zack and Tyson are on either side of me and the nervousness is fading into excitement. My shoulders feel lighter the further I make it on the field, which lets me lift my helmeted head a little taller. I could pass out or I could be completely fine–only time will tell.

I can't lose the game. Overtime or win. A perfect scenario.

People—technically teammates—I don't know are saying "Let's go, Blair" or the more aggressive "kick it down their throats" as we line up. I go where I was told and take a deep breath, waiting for the whistle and focusing on where the ball is going to be held. How many steps over. Where I kick. Everything my older brothers taught me when I was a kid.

I tune out as much as I can, feeling my breath in my chest, and my heart racing like it's got a marathon to run.

Breathe. In and out. In and out. Whistle. Snap. Approach. Kick.

And I fucking make it.

Six

Tyson

HAVING THE WOMAN OF my dreams make an extra point in an NFL game to win it was not on my bingo card today. Or maybe ever? But seeing it happen is going to make today impossible to beat.

You never know when your time is up as a professional athlete. One day, the sport is your main priority, and you sacrifice everything–your mind, body, and time–to perfect it. Many don't get to make the call, an injury or team management does it for them. While I've started to honestly think about when this should be for me, or when it could happen, today is the type of game that makes me want to play forever.

The team went wild. Running to her and jumping up and down, all while the crowd was screaming, making the arena feel like it was alive. I even saw Coach jump in the air and I don't know if anyone has seen him airborne in the last decade. When we got to the sidelines, Blair took her helmet off, and you could hear the confusion from the opposing teams' fans and players.

With Blair's extra point, the Cosmos pulled out the win. Coach brought her into the locker room and made sure everyone kept clothed until she was out. He gave her the game ball and told her not to miss her media appointment, which, that part may have been a joke, but she did all of it like a champ. She shook hands, met people, sat with Zack during his press conference, which is an experience in itself, and would've stayed as long as they wanted or needed her.

I could see it coming. Her crash. She'd been overwhelmed and pumped with adrenaline all day and I texted Joey–who was still losing his shit–planning our exit.

Now, we're at my apartment, eating takeout from four different restaurants—there's a little bit of everything, just how Blair likes it. Joey couldn't stay, needing to get back home to his pregnant wife, so the amount of food here is laughable.

"Did today really happen?" she asks while eating a forkful of caprese salad, a fried mozzarella stick in her other hand.

The same thought I've had more than once.

"You made history," I answer, popping a fried pickle in my mouth. Not a big fried food guy during the season, but this is one night where there are no rules. "You were fucking incredible."

"Stop. I'm going to get all hot again." She fans her cheeks, the ones that have been perpetually pink all day.

The doorbell buzzes and my doorman says there's a delivery. I meet him at the door and grab a bag—the one I knew was coming—and then he hands me a bottle of champagne with designer chocolates. I peek at the card and laugh when I see they're from Zack. That fucking guy.

"Well, these are both for you. Zack and Emilie, his wife, sent you the champagne and chocolates," I explain as I give her the card.

Blair beams as she reads–bubbly wine is definitely one of her favorite drinks. Maybe I should keep some here for when she's around?

Handing her the other bag, I say, "This one is from me."

She peeks in the bag and tips her head back with a groan. "My favorite pajamas. And leggings?" Blair looks down at her jeans and I can see the relief on her face. "How do you think of things like this?"

"When we were coming back, I knew you didn't have anything to change into. Knew you'd want to be comfortable."

She smiles at me in a slow way. Her eyes glisten, like she might cry, but even if she did, I know it's from the combination of the snacks and the idea of changing into stretchy pants.

"Thank you," Blair says, while peeling herself from the barstool to go change. "Feel free to open that bubbly for me."

There's a card with a sweet message from Emilie and Zack—also a jab about me probably not having flutes yet, but they would be right. I remove the foil and pop the top, grinning like an idiot when I think about the last few hours.

What a day.

I'm pouring the champagne into the expensive flutes—Zack does have great taste—as Blair walks out in the pajamas I had in my cart a few hours ago. I've probably seen her in every color or pattern imaginable.

Doesn't make her any less gorgeous.

"Did you know that the Cosmos have a women's locker room? With like... ridiculously nice products?" Her fingers pat her cheeks.

I tip my head back and laugh, "No, I didn't. But don't tell Zack, he'll ransack it." Handing her a flute, champagne fizzing to the top, I raise my barely-filled flute and say, "Cheers to you, Blair," and she clinks her glass to mine in response.

We each take a sip but then Blair doesn't stop—she downs the entire glass and stares at the table where the now empty flute sits. Her eyes don't meet mine and she doesn't move.

"So, there's a 99% chance I'm about to have a meltdown. I'm talking tears, weird laughing, it's all coming." Her voice is soft but twinged with the nervous laugh I'm familiar with.

Honestly, I'm surprised it took this long. Blair is so fucking good at managing things in the moment... she'll stretch herself thin until she's almost transparent. But, it eventually catches up.

"What do you need?"

AFTER A BOTTLE OF champagne, a few glasses of bourbon, equal amount of tears and nervous laughter, plus all the fancy chocolate she could stand, Blair is exhausted. She giggles into my chest as I reach down to pick her up and take her to bed.

She said I could take her home but that doesn't make any sense. After she told me she had tomorrow off at Embers and Ashes, I knew she'd stay here.

Her arms loop around my neck and it makes me hurt knowing how bad I want her. How amazing she is. Still can't believe no one has realized it yet—I always told myself these feelings would go away once she settled down with someone, but that has yet to happen. To be honest, we're trending in the wrong direction if the objective is less feelings.

I lean forward and set her on the bed, the side closest to the bathroom, pulling the covers up and over her.

"There's water on the table and side bathroom is right through there. I'll leave the light on," I say while her eyes roam over my face, a lopsided smirk on her full, pink lips.

Her lashes flutter, jet black, over her dark eyes. "You think of every-thing," her words drag. "How do you have so much room in there?" She puts her hands through my hair and I have to hold back from leaning into it. "So much room for thinking. So smart."

I let out a laugh while I get her situated. "You're smart, too. Lots of room in that brain." I jokingly tap her forehead.

"You're right. I do lots of thinking." Her voice rises and falls like she's reading a children's book.

Sitting back, I press, "Is that so? What do you think about?"

She tilts her head; her eyes are heavy and her lips tug on a corner. Blair takes in a slow breath, like she's trying to steady herself. "I always think you're going to kiss me. But you never do."

Her sleepy words turn me into a statue, sitting on the edge of the bed. She smiles at me for a few lazy seconds before turning on her side and settling into the pillows.

I sit there, frozen, until the sound of her deep breathing tells me she's asleep. Is my brain playing tricks on me? Did I really hear that?

I always think you're going to kiss me...but you never do.

Fuck, if she only knew how much I dreamt of it.

The Game Day Tribune

FROM THE STANDS TO THE STATS SHEET: BLAIR MILLER WINS IT ALL WITH ONE KICK

UPSTATE, N.Y.–The Upstate Cosmos ran out of kickers–and almost out of options–before they ran into Blair Miller.

In what might go down as the most chaotic pregame in NFL history, the Cosmos found themselves down not one, not two, but three kickers in four weeks. The final straw? Their emergency third-string popped an Achilles in warm ups.

According to the Cosmos' front office, they made some calls to see if anyone had any ideas on how to sign a kicker for the game but they came up empty.

But that's when long snapper and Super Bowl champ Zack Andersen came in. He suggested something absurd: see if anyone in the crowd could kick an extra point. If they find someone, put them on the roster.

It was supposed to be a wild idea. Probably a gimmick. Something to get fans excited before kickoff. Honestly, it's the Zack Andersen the Cosmos fans and team know and love.

Then Blair Miller was the last woman standing.

The Game Day Tribune

The thirty-year-old former Division I soccer star stepped up and crushed the competition in the impromptu pre-game contest. The fans expected her to win some swag, maybe tickets for a game, but certainly no one expected she'd see the sideline, dressed to play. With the score tied and six seconds left in regulation, the Cosmos punched in a touchdown–and needed one point to win the game.

They called her name. Granted, they did try going for two multiple times and were stuffed by the Kansas City Thunder defense.

One snap, one hold, one kick, and one chance to make history. Miller drilled it.

That single point sealed a Cosmos victory–and cemented her as the first woman to score in an NFL game, all on her first and only snap.

The Cosmos haven't said whether she's sticking around. But if you ask anyone in the locker room, she's already a legend.

Seven

Blair

LIFE COMES AT YOU fast, especially when you sort of wander onto an NFL roster for the rest of the season—or until they say they don't need you anymore. It's been three days and it's hard to even believe this is real life.

First, I now have a manager, Claire. She works with Willow—global superstar and love of my life even if she doesn't know it yet. Apparently, Tripp was raving about me to his girlfriend and Claire reached out to the Cosmos, offering to work with me for free. Weird kind of world when I think about how I'm playing football with Tripp, who's dating one of my favorite music artists of all time, and then we end up with the same manager.

Second, I could've paid her because my bank account is about to be in another tax bracket, but she insisted. Well, actually she told me, "You can buy the next one," like we were settling a tab at the bar.

When the Cosmos told me they'd pay me and get it all situated, I was expecting like a thousand dollars. Nope. The league minimum is well over eight hundred thousand dollars and that's what I'll get paid for being available for the Cosmos. I still don't believe it. There's no way this random extra point situation is going to put me in a different financial position—one I've dreamt of.

Third, I have practice. Since I still run a gym, I was able to get a modified Cosmos schedule, which has me working with special teams twice a week and then the final team walk through. They have a locker for me, in the women's locker room, and sent me a ridiculous amount of Cosmos gear—both ladies fit and unisex wear.

Lastly, I've had to put a pause on accepting gym memberships to Embers and Ashes. It only took a few hours after I made the extra point for my identity to be revealed and the gym to be inundated with people wanting to join. A dream come true, but also scary as fuck. So far, everyone has been respectful and there for the right reasons. A few people have asked me for photos and I'm more than happy to do that.

If I'm being honest with myself, it's a nice distraction. I've not seen Tyson since I made up an excuse to leave his apartment too early after staying over due to my loose lips the night before. Honestly? It's kind of Zack's fault—he sent that delicious champagne, and when that was gone, the bourbon was just as smooth, and next thing you know...

I always think you're going to kiss me...

I'm a fucking cliché and it's embarrassing. To my bones, I can't believe those words made it out of my brain. Even with the drinks, it was like I was having an out of body experience—floating above the two of us—as I casually told Tyson, one of my best friends and favorite people in the world, how I thought about him kissing me.

I mean, it was true. But it wasn't something I intended to share. The thought of him putting an end to the possibility of us exploring something more is enough to have me hold onto this secret with white knuckles.

I'm supposed to be one of the guys—I'm literally his teammate now—and the man has never once put a single move on me. It's never been like that.

The pit in my stomach opens up, like my journal pages are flipping to the worn handwriting—the lines where I wondered about ending up with Tyson. The secret I've kept to myself.

He's always had this pull to me. Ever since we met, he's been able to take the most run of the mill things and make them feel special. His jersey is strewn over a chair, and it brings me back to a night in college.

The floor might be sticky and the beer might be warm, but this is the most fun I'd had at a house party in a minute.

Not surprising, considering Tyson and I were tucked in a corner, seemingly in our own little world. He laughed like he means it, like you were the only one in on the joke, and somewhere between his dumb impressions and the way he always saved me a drink at these things, I'd started looking at him longer than I should.

I liked him. Quietly. Stupidly.

And he didn't have a clue.

I was mid-thought when Tyson elbowed me. "Hey," he said, nodding toward the far end of the room. "Flannel over there is giving you heart-eyes."

I blinked and followed his gaze. Sure enough—tall guy, lean build, sharp jaw. Cute. Definitely looking. Probably on the basketball team.

"He's been staring since you walked in," Tyson added, a crooked grin playing at his lips. "Should probably put him out of his misery."

I smirked and took a sip from my drink. "Maybe I'm good here?" I willed him to forget about anyone else looking over here. At me. At him.

"I know I'm a blast." He puffed up, mockingly, then tilted his head toward Flannel Guy again. "But he's not bad. You should go talk to him."

His voice was light. Easy. Like he wasn't sending me toward something that made my stomach twist—but not in a good way. I hesitated, gaze drifting back to the guy. He lit up when our eyes met. I tried scanning the room for anyone who might be looking for their opening with Tyson and my stomach bottomed out.

Tyson nudged me gently. "You got this."

I glanced up at him one more time, searching for something in his face—hesitation, jealousy, anything—but he was already looking away, sipping his drink like it was just any other night.

So I smiled. Bright, fake, and practiced.

And then I lifted my hand and waved at the guy. I hated the way my heart sank as he started walking over.

The same pit reopens when I think about last night. He's not something I'm willing to risk. He's not even a chip I'd consider wagering. But maybe someone should've reminded the version of myself from the other night of that very sentiment. The one that let him carry her, in the pajamas he had delivered, into his bed, which smelled like him—all leathery and clean—and then just spit out that horrific line about kissing.

I know this is one of those things that will race through my mind for the next twenty years when I try to fall asleep. Here's to anxiety and it keeping track of your most cringeworthy moments—the scoreboard you can't run from.

Think about something else. This can't be what's on my mind as I walk into my first practice. Standing in front of my locker, I stretch my neck from side to side as my eyes fixate on my locker name plate. *Blair Miller. #7. Special teams.*

I catch my reflection and step closer to the mirror. My typical longline sports bra and high waisted legging workout uniform are nowhere to be found. The leggings could stay, but a Cosmos branded quarter zip covers my top half.

Facing the mirror, I fixate on the outline of my body. I've always been sort of square shaped, straight up and down. When I was younger, and before I knew better, I'd do all of these fad exercises or supersets trying to grow that perfect peach shaped ass everyone was after. I'd undereat to the point of lightheadedness being the norm and push myself harder than anyone ever should at the gym.

Figuring out how to properly move, fuel, and build my body is something that completely changed my life. I fell in love with it—putting the pieces of the puzzle together. It also saved me from myself. It wasn't until I was in a great place that I recognized how bad my mental health really was before—how I'd been living with depression and anxiety without ever knowing it had a name.

I thought everyone hated themselves the way I did. Or thought through almost every step, or possibility, of a social interaction before it happened. It's not that I don't do those things anymore—depression is one of the most consistent things in an inconsistent world—but I can check in with my body, my brain, and do my best to give it what it needs.

I don't always get it right—I think to myself as I start to scrutinize the body in front of me. My hand reaches across my chest and squeezes the space between my neck and my shoulder.

Your arms are too big.

You look manly.

Who would find this attractive?

To be fair, I didn't come up with these insults. These are things people have said to me, for almost my entire life, in some way shape or form.

Some of the most vivid memories I have of my dad are him yelling at my mom for letting me do things with the boys. *This isn't for girls. Girls shouldn't do that. Boys don't like girls who beat them, or talk too loud, or have dirt under their fingernails.* He left when I was twelve, but he did a whole lifetime of damage before he finally packed his bags.

We were better off but it still hurt. My mom was never quite the same—it was like he took pieces of her she didn't know he had access to. There weren't many times that I can ever remember them being happy, but it was like there was hope that he would be the man she fell in love with—a spark waiting for kindling. He left and never looked back. And the last time I heard from him was a birthday card on my eighteenth birthday.

I can practically feel my confidence slipping away, one internal insult at a time. My belly tenses and I take a breath, feeling the stretch of my lungs. My brain attempts to build up the wall that lets me scale it and push past the thoughts.

I'm only a couple steps from the locker room when a familiar face spots me, grinning as he asks, "You ready for your first practice?"

Dylan Peterson, kicking specialist for the Upstate Cosmos. He helped me with a crash course on practice kicks at the game and treated me like an athlete, as soon as he heard my current training plan. I liked him right away.

"I think so. Kind of have that same feeling when you're walking into a group fitness class when it's something you've never done." I clap my hands, letting them swing to my sides. "So, like I'm about to make a complete ass of myself."

A tiny laugh sneaks out, making me feel a little better. "Small crew today. Everyone is doing skill specific work. That means we'll start in the gym, see where you're at with some lifting benchmarks, and then it will just be you, me and a long snapper for some kicking drills."

When Dylan found out I owned a gym, was a college athlete, and was borderline obsessed with a routine, he almost dropped to his knees to thank whatever god he prayed to. I wasn't what they expected, in more than one way, and it was like I could watch his eyes go from 'this might be a wild PR stunt' to 'this could be something legit for the team.'

"Plus, some of the trainers are women, which means you won't be the only girl in the club today."

A smile lifts a corner of my lips, the competitive fire I'm accustomed to lighting in my muscles, and I reply, "Believe me, I've never been afraid to be the only girl."

We walk into the gym and I have to consciously keep my jaw from dragging on the floor. I don't know why I assumed the gym would be a bit dated and smell like feet—maybe too many rom-coms where the male lead is a coach or player—but that isn't the case. The space is open, modern, with lighting that would serve even the pickiest of influencers.

Shoes pounding treadmills, stationary bikes whirring, and weights being racked compose the soundtrack and it wraps around my shoulders like a cozy blanket. There's nothing like the fine-tuned machine of a well-run, and used gym.

The thing I may be most surprised by is the energy. The vibe. Whatever you decide to call it, but it feels supportive, strong, and encouraging. I feel like I was waiting for competitiveness and egos to gag me—I almost texted Tyson asking him about this exact thing but couldn't bring myself to hit send.

Embarrassment hits my cheeks for only a second before Dylan asks, "You ready to get some work done?"

I nod and shake out my hands.

Work. A task. The gym. I can definitely do this.

Well, probably.

Tyson

DID BLAIR JUST GIVE me finger guns?

We're doing our walk through for the home game tomorrow against The Serpents. That means Blair has had her first practice, plus a special teams day, and I've heard from her zero times. I thought that this whole bizarre thing would bring us closer together.

Maybe not.

And the first time she sees me, she gives me finger guns?

I fall into the task at hand. We're in the film room discussing the team we're up against tomorrow. Honestly, they've had a rough season—only winning two of their last five games—and this should be a fairly easy Cosmos win. But while we have Blair to kick extra points, we still don't have a field goal kicker.

I think the team is afraid to have her try and fail–they don't want any dings to her confidence. Field goal attempts are different from extra points–more difficult, with lots of variables. So, the only film we fixate on from our previous game is our piss-poor attempt at two point conversions after scoring a touchdown. Not good.

I look over and see Zack shoulder to shoulder with Blair—her hair is tied back in a short ponytail, some of the chocolate locks falling on the nape of her neck. They're watching film and going through a playbook, giving her a crash course on what she doesn't know. Which, honestly, probably isn't a lot.

Blair has always been into sports, ever since I've known her, and according to her brothers, since she could keep up with them. It was never enough to know the rules; she wanted to understand everything—the positions, plays, and strategy.

She's not one to half-ass anything. It's something I love about her.

Something. On top of the *many* other things.

I rub my hands over my face, covering any of the red hitting my cheeks, because this isn't the place to think about the woman I've been in love with for a decade. The woman who found a way to tie herself to me, in a way I didn't even know was there, the first day we met.

College kids and driving in the snow were a horrible combination. Walking in it wasn't much better.

She came out of nowhere—buried under at least three bags, worn-in sneakers on her feet, no winter boots in sight. One second she's upright, the next she was tilting towards the bumper of a silver Jeep—about to slide right under.

I lunged, catching her around the waist before she could face-plant. "Got you," I said, hauling her back onto steady feet.

Her eyes went wide, sunlight reflecting off pools of honey, and then she let out a strangled laugh. "Cool. Totally fine. Just practicing my new stunt routine. Thought I'd debut it here in the parking lot."

I grinned, still holding her arm. "Not bad. Needs a little less... death-defying."

Her cheeks were pink—not just from the cold. She yanked one bag higher on her shoulder, like it might distract from the fact I just kept her from eating asphalt. "Guess I should've charged admission. Front row seats and everything."

I shook my head, fighting a laugh. "Now, that's a way to help pay for college." I reached for one of her bags before she could stop me. "Probably should wear winter boots or something if you're going to be a pack mule. A simple suggestion."

"Not a pack mule. Just a student athlete trying to make it to classes, practice, and the weight room. You get it." She shrugged, her eyes locking on mine.

"Cheerleading?" I asked, given the whole stunt routine comment.

The laugh that skipped through her was vibrant and quick, her breath a white cloud in front of her lips. "Soccer. But I am flattered that, from this interaction, you think I'm that coordinated." She smiled, and it was hard not to match her. "And I'm Blair."

Not knowing where we were headed, I fell into step beside her. "Tyson. And I play football." I gave her information she didn't ask for, and then something clicked. "Does that mean you're going to the mixer thing tonight?"

"Yes. My boyfriend plays basketball. We'll be there later." She stopped in front of the dorm doors. She reached for her bags, so I passed one over and grabbed the door for her.

Trying to drown the sudden disappointment, I forced a casual, "Cool. I'll see you there."

She tipped her chin to me. "See you there."

Later that night, I saw her again. Hair down in loose chocolate curls, that easy smile already aimed my direction. When she spotted me, she gave a little wave.

And right then, I knew—it was the start of something.

Fuck. I'm in trouble. I've always been in trouble.

I chug the water sitting in front of me, trying to restart my brain, and a pinch of loneliness makes it hard to swallow. For the first time in a while, I feel like I'm alone even though the room is crowded. Just me.

And the thoughts that never seem to quit.

"I FEEL LIKE WE'RE about to celebrate your eightieth birthday or something," Teague teases as he slides into the restaurant booth. "We're definitely here for the early bird special," he muses while looking at his watch.

"If I was turning eighty, you'd be eighty-five," I poke at my older brother as we open the menu. Since tomorrow is game day, I've got a curfew and a hotel room to get back to. Even if it's a home game, the team stays together—aiming to keep everyone focused and in bed at a decent time.

He lets out a laugh, one that makes me feel like we're back home. We've always gotten along, for as long as I can remember. Teague was always so excited to show off his little brother who got bigger than him really fast. Not saying we didn't bicker or torture each other, but the fights were always short lived and we were quick to make up and get into whatever was next.

Teague moved to New York once he graduated from college. He played college football and was damn good, but not good enough for the NFL—especially when an Achilles injury took him out his senior year. The thing my parents always told us was that we could play football if we got good grades. When we played college football, they basically asked us for a blood pact when it came to finishing and graduating with a degree. We both did that—no pact required—and while I got the NFL roster spot, Teague is a fucking genius and works in data analysis at some tech company in the city.

"No, I love it. I'll be home to help with bedtime." He smiles, genuine and bright. Teague is married to his college sweetheart and they have a little girl, who is going to be two in a couple of months.

He loves being a dad and I'm fucking happy he gave me a niece to love on. Being closer to them was a big perk when I got the news about getting traded.

Once we order our food and I quickly sign something for a fan who spotted me, Teague presses, "How much fun are you having with Blair? That has to be wild." He drinks from his pint glass.

I take a long swig from my iced tea. "It's fun. That day was really something."

Teague's look is long and pointed, brows squished as he gives me a side-eye. "Seriously, keep it down. Wouldn't want you to start a scene with all that enthusiasm you've got there." He whispers loudly, sarcasm flying, hands pushing down on something invisible in front of him.

"No, it's cool." I shrug my shoulders. "She's out here doing something no one's ever done. Happy to be part of it." I try to make it sound like I'm not talking about something like a loose paperclip at the bottom of a drawer, but even I know it falls flat.

Teague leans back into the booth, crossing his arms. He slowly shakes his head as he presses his lips together, before they morph into a grin. And then he's laughing to himself, eyes glancing at the ceiling.

What the hell?

"Care to share with the group?" I try to sound light and easy going but if anyone can read it as bullshit, it's Teague.

"You're finally going to come clean. I can feel it." He claps his hands together, rubbing them before leaning forward on the table.

I take another drink, my brows lifted, and when I don't say anything, he rolls his eyes.

"About Blair."

Playing as dumb as I can, I respond, "What about her?"

Shaking his head, he whispers, "Come on. We talk about everything... including how you think this might be your last contract in the NFL, but you're really going to make me say it?" His hands are flat on the table, his wedding ring clinking at the contact, and he lets the silence run between us. "Blair. You love her. You've always been in love with her. Maybe you've always known, maybe not, but now it's different."

Choosing to ignore the one time we talked about how I felt my time was running out for the NFL, I reply, "That's quite the theory you have there." I respond without catching his eyes, because I'm this close to cracking. I feel like the bastard knows it, too.

"Tell me I'm wrong and I'll drop it. Or, I could help you."

He's right; we've never had this conversation. When I came home and told my family about Blair, everyone jumped to the idea of her being my girlfriend, but I quickly corrected them. We were always *just friends*. And then she was my *best* friend. And then she was coming home with me during some of the holidays, and my family loved her. My parents always told me they'd take Blair any way they could get her.

Teague asked me about it once. It was our junior year, the third Thanksgiving I'd brought her home for, and she fell asleep in my bed. I was in the hallway, grabbing blankets so I could make a bed on the floor, just not wanting to leave her side. Teague saw me, peeked his head in my room, and asked me point blank: are you in love with this girl or something? I scoffed, shook my head, and tried to convince my older brother he had no idea what he was talking about.

But deep down, I knew I was. I always had these feelings for Blair that were difficult to characterize. From the first day I saved her, even the night I saw her with her boyfriend at the athlete mixer, there was something about her I couldn't shake.

Maybe it's because I'm ready, or dying, to talk about it. Figure out what to do.

I let out a breath and come to terms with the fact that I'm caught. "What would you suggest?"

"I fucking knew it. All these years, I knew it!" Excitement fills his face and it makes me want to punch him in the arm so he'll shut up, while also getting out a notepad and pen and taking whatever advice he can give me. "What's the issue? You're back in the same place and you're going to be regularly seeing each other."

The air hardly fills my lungs, and I can barely look at him when I say, "I don't know. She's never made a move or said anything. But neither have I. And now it's the football thing." I know I'm not making much sense, no matter how much Teague is trying to keep up. "After the game, she was at my place. She had some drinks and I was putting her to bed, all platonic like, and she said something. For the first time."

"You're actually killing me, you know that? Get on with it. What'd she say?" His voice matches the smirk he wears, glowing eyes to match.

"'I always think you're going to kiss me. But you never do.' That's what she said."

He blinks, eyes wide, "And then..."

"And then she fell asleep. That was it. And we haven't talked since."

He tilts his head, eyes squinted. "You mean to tell me that you didn't kiss her? After she practically begged you to?"

"There was no begging."

"Why would she say that to you?" he prompts.

"I don't know. I'm trying to figure it out." I rub my forehead with my fingers, staring intently at the table in front of me, like it's about to tell me the answers to all my questions.

"Tyson, are you kidding me? I know I'm supposed to be the smart one, but damn. She wanted you to kiss her!"

"Maybe she didn't finish her thought? Maybe it was supposed to be... I always think you're going to kiss me, but you never do AND THANK GOD."

He gives me his best dad look, one he'll get good use out of for the next ten years. "Tyson. That's quite the fucking jump. Also, why do you leap to the worst possible scenario?"

Shrugging, I answer, "I can't help it. It's the first place I went."

"I don't know why you do that. Not only with Blair, but in general. You're the nice guy, in the best way. You're thoughtful and are always willing to lend a hand, but you don't think it makes you worth it? Not to mention you never put yourself first." His voice drifts at the end.

I understand what he's saying but I can't make it make sense. Doing things for others comes naturally to me but I don't expect it from anyone. I think much more about my worth than I care to admit. It doesn't help that my job is centered around the same concept, of course under a different approach and lens, but it's all *what can you give the organization* or *are you worth what we're paying you.*

When Teague realizes I'm not going to bite—only one existential crisis topic at a time—he continues, "Back to Blair. It's time to talk about it."

"That would be way too logical," I joke.

The truth is... I'm terrified. Afraid to ask, afraid to get an answer, afraid to put what we have at risk. When it's out in the open, no more question marks, there's no going back.

Teague's face softens, like he can read my mind. To be honest, some days I wonder if he can. "You know you should talk to her. No matter what happens, isn't it better to know? Once and for all?" My big brother's voice hits me in the chest because I know he's right.

Fuck.

The Game Day Tribune

COSMOS CRUISE PAST SERPENTS, CONTINUE WILD RIDE THROUGH NFL'S STRANGEST SPECIAL TEAMS SEASON

UPSTATE, N.Y.–The Upstate Cosmos made easy work of the Seattle Serpents on Sunday afternoon, notching a 27-10 victory in what has become one of the most bizarre and compelling seasons in NFL special teams' history.

A week removed from nearly missing the league's ninety-minute roster window without an active kicker–before signing Blair Miller, the first woman ever on an NFL roster–the Cosmos prevailed once again without a single field goal. While Miller made headlines last week for drilling a game-winning extra point under extreme pressure, this week was all about testing the adjustments to the run game, and they delivered.

The Cosmos went 3-for-3 on two-point conversions, a surprising move that their head coach later said was "part strategy, part identity crisis."

Miller added her second career point in the 4th quarter, calmly drilling an extra point to cap off a twelve play drive. While it wasn't a game-winner, the sideline erupted–more out of appreciation than urgency.

The Game Day Tribune

The Cosmos' erratic approach to special teams has become the talk of the league, and honestly, all leagues. The Cosmos have opened the door to something unique; maybe a little risky, but it's almost impossible not to cheer for Blair Miller. Within two hours of the Cosmos putting her jersey in the online store, they were sold out.

With Miller growing more confident and the offense finding rhythm on two-point tries, the Cosmos might just be proving that consistency is overrated–as long as you're scoring.

Nine

Blair

THE UNANSWERED TEXTS ABOVE this one twist my gut. Things with Tyson have been murky and weird—I hate it. I gave him finger guns when I saw him at walk through like an idiot, and then acted like I didn't know he was waiting for me after I was lifting in the Cosmos gym. We've been acting like acquaintances and not like we've known each other for a third of our lives.

To be fair, I fear I've fallen into a completely different level of overwhelm. Everything is fine... or maybe I've said it enough that I wholeheartedly believe it. Embers and Ashes is in a great spot, but I don't get to spend as much time there as I'd like. Business has never been better, but I miss it.

It's where I love to work out, where my body feels the strongest. The Cosmos gym is definitely adequate, but it's not the same. The time away from my gym, my staff, even my favorite coffee shop is throwing me. Not to mention the new rule I set for myself about staying off the internet. Doom scrolling isn't any fun when you wind up in a hole that's talking about you.

My phone buzzes as I put on the devil horns to round out my costume.

"Oooh, this is a direction for the team Halloween party," Mags croons as her face fills my phone screen.

Propping my phone up, I step back so she can see the entire costume.

"Wait. Are you an egg?"

"I'm a deviled egg." I gesture down to my full outfit as Mags claps and laughs from a thousand miles away. I think she's about to play a Women's Tennis Association tournament in Japan—sometimes your best friend has to work and her job takes her all over the world.

Her laugh is contagious and I tilt my head to the ceiling, my shoulders shaking. "The theme this year is a Punny Halloween. Tyson promised me that everyone plays along." I take a drink from the coffee cup I've refilled maybe one too many times today.

"Well, this is stellar. Grade A costume choice." She smiles, her face close to the screen. "I'm glad I was able to get a hold of you, and seeing your outfit is a definite bonus."

My chest squeezes knowing I've not been able to take a FaceTime from her in what feels like weeks. I know she doesn't hold it against me, but it's one of those things that makes me feel off kilter. Maggie feels like a staple that helps keep me together.

"I know. I can't seem to get my footing."

Maggie shakes her head. "You and Tyson still acting like you didn't talk about kissing the other night?" I can feel her side-eye all the way in America.

"Yes. Complete avoidance. An effective tactic, if I do say so myself."

"Any thoughts about what you meant?" Her words are pointed, in the sharp way they tend to get when she's asking me questions about Tyson. She never pushes too hard, but she knows more than she'd ever let on. And that's why I love her the way I do.

"No, not really."

Lie.

Did I fixate about the fact he had my favorite type of pajamas delivered to his place? After he ordered all my favorite foods? Yes and yes. More often than I'd admit to anyone. But I'm also going over the part where I talked about him kissing me and he did absolutely nothing. It's all jumbled and on top of each other. He's one of the most thoughtful people I've ever had the chance to know, and he can make you feel like you're the only person in a room even if it's wall to wall crowded.

But maybe I'm truly one of the guys. He doesn't look at me like someone he could fall in love with. The things he does for me, he does for everyone, in one way or another.

"And even if I did, I'll tell you when it's the wrong time to have conversations like this... when you work together. In one of the most public ways."

Truth.

Mags nods her head in understanding. "I get that. But you can't walk around it forever. Something's gotta give, eventually, right?"

"Let's just hope it's not when I'm dressed up like a fucking deviled egg at an NFL team party because that would be a special type of torture."

TYSON OFFERED TO PICK me up but I pretended like I didn't see his message until it was too late. I'm not avoiding him—well, maybe I am—but I'm just hoping for a few minutes to get my head on straight.

I was so preoccupied with what I was going to say to Tyson that I sort of walked into Zack's like I'd been here a hundred times before. The stress and nerves of showing up to a teammate's house for the first time were nowhere to be found.

Looking around, relief hits my shoulders and shrinks me down to my appropriate height when I see everyone following the punny theme. I see players dressed like an F-Bomb, a pig in a blanket, and even Fifty Shades of Gray by putting paint chips on a black shirt.

Thank god.

"And this is how you do a punny Halloween!" Zack lifts a cup in my direction; everyone follows suit, and while they all drink I'm glad I decided to bring the plastic pitchfork to really round out the whole ensemble.

Zack is dressed in a graduation robe and cap, chocolate chip cookies fastened to his front.

I nod in understanding. "You're one smart cookie," I point at him with the pitchfork. Zack points back at me before jokingly bowing in front of me. Someone yells for him at the door and I'm left alone.

This year, the party's at Zack's—it sounds like the host rotates each year and whoever hosts picks the theme. I'm pretty sure this floor could fit six of my studio apartments. With floor-to-ceiling windows, and tucked in right on the edge of the city, there's a skyline view of New York that's hard to beat. No matter how many times I've seen it, it still makes me feel some type of way. Like, something so individualized can be so gorgeous together. A bunch of random buildings, lights, windows, silhouettes—they have no business sparkling the way they do when the sun goes down.

"It's pretty, isn't it?" Tyson's voice cuts through the sound of the party.

He's wearing an orange shirt with the pi symbol on the front. *Pumpkin pie.* As soon as it registers, he leans forward and points to his cheeks.

"Wait, are those temporary tattoos?" There's a little pumpkin on the top of one of his cheeks and a pumpkin pie on the other.

He laughs, one of my favorite sounds, and says, "Zack told me that since I didn't have a full costume, it'd only be appropriate with a little extra oomph. Apparently, this is what he meant." Ty shrugs, playing it off like he doesn't love to go all in on a theme.

The smirk which tugs at one side of his mouth does something to me. Something it shouldn't, because I'm fairly certain that melting into a puddle, thinking of that smirking mouth on me, at a team party, isn't it.

I need a drink.

I find the bar, tip my head towards it, and Tyson follows me. There's a list of featured cocktails, because why wouldn't there be, and I act like I'm enthralled by the list. Tyson's hip bumps into mine as he leans on the bar.

Once I've got a drink that's supposed to be vampire blood—champagne and raspberry liqueur—Tyson leads me to a group of guys. While I've loosely met everyone and seen them at games and at practice, it's hard to get to know this many people. Teams usually have months to do something I've tried to do in a few weeks.

A pit of nerves starts to open in my core—like walking into the first day of school when you don't know anyone. Fuck, does the Halloween costume make this better or worse? Before I have time to get into it, the standing table erupts with a collective "hey" and a few "Blairs!" The excitement eases my nerves and I settle in, taking a sip of my cocktail, as teammates reintroduce themselves and let me into the group.

"Thank god we have the day off tomorrow," Tyson groans, taking in his teammates—some of whom have had a bit to drink. He takes a slow drink of his beer, his Adam's apple bobbing with the swig.

Clapping and cheers come from the door—someone else must be here. I crane my neck to see Benny White, the multi-million dollar kicker for the Cosmos who broke his leg during the first game, sidelining him for this season. He's wearing a blue button-up dress shirt and has a Dunder Mifflin decal on a crutch—he's Michael Scott when he steps on the George Foreman grill from The Office. Solid choice.

Tyson stands, I follow suit, and soon Benny is slowly making his way over. When our eyes meet, a flash of recognition hits him. We may have never met but we both know who the other is.

"Blair Miller. I've been dying to meet you," A crutch props him up under his arm pit and he offers his hand. His voice bubbles with energy and it's like an out of body experience—an NFL player who is dying to meet me? Who would've thought?

I put my hand in his, shaking it, and smile back at him. "Likewise. I was so sorry to hear about your injury. How are you feeling?" I glance down at the still-casted leg.

"Better, now that I know they have someone who can step in. I wish you could've seen me on the phone with Dylan when he called to tell me about you. I thought it was a joke until I saw it for myself. How the hell did you learn to do that?"

"I did play college soccer, but this is all the product of older brothers and a mean competitive streak." I shrug my shoulders.

He laughs and the way he looks at me has me feeling lighter. It's like his face is filled with gratitude, and maybe a bit of relief. I get it—if I was a key part of my team's strategy and not able to deliver... that would eat me alive.

"I'd like their addresses so I can send them a thank you gift. You're a solid add to the team. You guys know each other from college, right?" He gestures between me and Tyson.

Turning to look at Tyson almost turns my mouth to sandpaper. His blue eyes dart to mine and they're the color of the ocean crashing on the coast—the one you dream of. I take a sip of my vampire blood drink, realizing it's practically empty, and answer, "Yes. We've known each other a long time."

Before Tyson can jump in, someone stands too close to me, hitting my hip with theirs. He's looking down at a cell phone until he realizes he bumped into me. Awkwardly, his eyes find my face for a brief second, before they go back to his phone, and to me again for an enthusiastic double take.

"Oh look, you're dressed like my ex-wife." He jokes but it lands flat. He's wearing a suit that's too expensive to be a costume and he's the only one laughing.

"She's a deviled egg..." Tyson says, almost in a question, his cheeks scrunched in the same confusion we're all feeling, the temporary pumpkin and pie tattoos crinkling.

The man gives Tyson a glimpse of a look and returns to his phone, "Oh. Well, the devil part. You get it." His fingers move over the keyboard and he doesn't look back up until too many long seconds have passed between us. "Hey, you're that girl." He snaps his fingers at me and I don't know where the strength comes from but I hold everything back not to give him a 'what the fuck' look. "Claire?"

No. My blood starts to boil but before I can correct him, everyone around me says, "Blair."

"Right, Blair," he says while looking back to his phone. The man doesn't even have the audacity to apologize or make eye contact. "Well, thanks for keeping this guy's spot warm. He's going to be back before you know it." He grabs Benny's shoulder, jostling him a little harder than I think is okay for someone on crutches.

I press my lips together, trying to keep my face blank, even though this man doesn't deserve it. It's like he's marking his territory. Part of me finds it hard to believe he didn't know my name. He's just that special kind of asshole who can't even lean into common human decency, like getting someone's name right.

"This is, uh, Oscar, my agent. Zack invited him." Benny's voice drops an octave and enough decibels to pick up on his discomfort. And if that didn't do it, certainly his eyes finding the floor would.

I hold back a laugh as Zack stands behind Oscar, shaking his head, face etched with an expression, making it clear he didn't really invite him. Tyson sees Zack and coughs, covering his mouth with his hand, clearly hiding the same reaction.

I put my hand out, because this isn't the first toxic man I've met and won't be the last. "Blair Miller. From what I know, lots of people know that name. I think I sold the most jerseys this week?" I look around, waiting for the guys to hype me up. Hoping. Otherwise, this would be really embarrassing.

But they do.

They clap, laugh, and cheer me on. Even Benny is throwing his head back, mouth open in a full belly laugh. No one expected me to say anything... fuck, I didn't expect it either. Maybe it's the cocktails, maybe it's the guys treating me like I'm one of them, or maybe it's this guy's bad attitude?

I laugh with my teammates as Oscar refuses to look at me. And you know what?

Good.

Ten

Tyson

Holy shit. Blair holding her own? Being the only woman in the room? Sign me up. Zack asked if we should include spouses or partners, so Blair would have other women to meet, and I told him it wasn't necessary. She loves contributing to a team and tonight was a perfect way to spend more time with the guys.

Looks like I was right, and it's been a blast watching them get to know her—seeing her come out of her shell. Even with Oscar's antics, that smart ass knew her name, there's no way he couldn't. But Blair coming out swinging with the jersey sales? Fuck, that was good.

I've heard enough about Oscar to know he's someone I'd never consider hiring. I'm fairly certain I heard talk in the locker room about Benny moving on at the end of the season which would be quite the statement given he won't play the rest of the year.

Can't believe he showed up like he's one of us. Clearly, he's not.

Oscar made some lame excuse to leave shortly after Blair put him in his place and Benny made sure to apologize for his behavior, even though it's not his to own.

The group has naturally split up, with some guys going to the pool table, others grabbing a controller to play video games. Zack's place is perfect for something like this because there's space, activities, and places for people to fall into.

Blair gazes out the floor to ceiling windows, the skyline sparkling on the other side of the glass.

"Want to go out on the balcony?" I almost expect her to say no since it feels like she's been avoiding me for days.

She nods, holding onto her fresh cocktail with two hands. Her hair swishes when she walks, almost touching her shoulders, but not quite. I hold the door open and nod to the corner, where I know there's a small outdoor fire table.

I almost drop to my knees when we see all the chairs empty—no one besides the two of us. Instead, I let Blair pick a spot and then drape a blanket over her lap.

A long breath slips from her mouth. "I hope no one's mad about that whole thing with Oscar. I didn't need to say the thing about the jerseys—" Her eyes catch mine and they're glowing in the firelight.

"Are you kidding? They loved it!" I lean forward, resting my forearms on my knees as I look at her through the flames on the table. "And yes you did. He was being a dick. If you didn't say it, someone else would've."

"Maybe you. Not sure if anyone else would care." She takes a slow drink of the bubbly cocktail, eyes looking up at the stars.

There it is. Or part of it.

Nodding, I say, "They would've. Believe me. You think these guys don't know you saved our ass? That we're not lucky to have you? They do. Honestly, everyone's jealous of Zack because he gets to spend the most time with you and he *loves* to brag about how funny you are. How you're friends."

Her shoulders soften with each word. "Ugh. I'm sorry. I don't know why I'm being like this. All needy and annoying."

"You're not *that* needy." I try to joke, to get her to loosen up. "Is that why you've been sort of radio silent?" I turn her insecurity into needing clarity for my own.

Her head tilts and I'm afraid for what's going to come next. How she's embarrassed she said anything about kissing me. How she could never see me that way.

"This is your job. Your dream. And it feels like I'm being thrown in and—" Her words are quick, almost falling from her lips like she's running out of time. "I don't want to ruin this for you or make it difficult or let anyone down—"

"Blair. Breathe." I don't continue until I see her chest rise and fall, slow and intentional. "First things first, you can't consider everyone. There's not a way to make them all happy. Quite literally impossible. All I can tell you is that the team loves having you, everyone I've talked to, at least."

She smiles but it makes me want to reach out and pull her to me. It's got this sadness to it. It hurts me that she thinks she's overstepping. That I don't want her here.

"And, if I ever did something to make you feel like this was negatively impacting me, I'm sorry. You being here? It makes it better. How many people get to do something like this with their best friend?"

A little laugh breaks through her sad exterior, cracking it a bit. "Best friends. I love when you say that."

"I mean it."

It still feels like she isn't getting it. My heart thumps in my chest and I'm thankful for the wind breezing through the leaves, falling from their branches—anything to mask the sound because I swear she could probably hear it.

I have to give her something.

"When they called me about the trade, do you know the first thing I thought of?" Her dark honey eyes are on me, and it's like a rope is tightening around my chest, making it hard to catch my breath. "You. How we were going to be in the same place for the first time since college. It wasn't the money. The moving logistics. Sadness for leaving my current home. Missing the guys. It was how I was going to finally be closer to you."

"Tyson—"

"So, when you say you think you're stepping on my toes, or anything like that, you're wrong. And I know you're the one who typically needs to be right, but you're not going to win this one."

"Okay." She agrees and it's not what I expected. Her voice is soft like velvet. "You're right. I'm wrong."

My eyebrows push into my forehead. "Wow, I know that must've been hard." I take a drink of my beer—the same one I've been nursing for an hour. The fire crackles between us, throwing light across her face. She's close enough that her warmth competes with the flames.

It feels like a now or never moment. If there's something I wanted to bring up, or say, here's my chance. Every second I don't say something, the air tightens—like the night itself is waiting. My hand trembles around the bottle, so I curl it into a fist against my knee.

"I want to ask you something but I'm afraid."

Blair's eyes lift to mine, dark lashes framing, and she presses her lips together. "Afraid of what?" She doesn't lean back. She leans in—just a fraction—and that tiny movement nearly unravels me.

"The answer. Changing things."

Her lips part, like she's ready to speak, but no words come. She exhales instead—slow—like she's trying to steady herself too. Her fingers stretch toward the bottle sitting between us, and for a heartbeat, the back of her hand grazes mine. A different kind of fire rips through me.

"The night at my place after your first game. You said something. I tried forgetting you said it but I can't." My knuckles strain white against my skin as I rub my hands together. My chest feels too small for the words pushing up my throat. "'I always think you're going to kiss me. But you never do.'"

She takes in a breath, holds it, and looks around before letting it out.

"I did say that. I remember saying it."

Here goes nothing. Everything.

"What did you mean?"

"I didn't mean to make things weird between us," she whispers, her head falling into her hands and staying there like she's afraid to meet my eyes and see what this is doing to me.

Before I can talk myself out of it, I'm walking to her. I reach for her arm and pull her up until we're toe-to-toe, her breath hitting my chin.

"That isn't what I asked. What *did* you mean?" I look down at her and the woman who usually barrels through life like she can't be knocked down looks like she's one wrong word from shattering. Same as me.

"I meant exactly what I said." Her voice is matter of fact but the tiny tremor beneath it ruins her poker face. "I always think you're going to kiss me. But you never do. Well, actually, I'd probably swap always for sometimes but it's exactly what it sounds like."

She lifts her chin, daring me to do something about it. Terrified I will. Terrified I won't.Blair emphasizes the change of phrase with her hands and I catch them before she can tuck them away, my fingers wrapping around hers. The backs of them are cold from the October air. She doesn't pull back.

She bites her lip and her body tilts that tiny, telling inch closer. "But you don't have to answer it. Or respond. Or I don't even know at this point. I know we've only ever been friends—"

I interrupt her, the words tripping out like I've held them too long. "Do you think about me kissing you?"

My gaze drops to her mouth—those crimson lips curved like they're already winning a game I didn't know we were playing, perfectly matching her devil horns and the complexity she brings with her.

My heart doesn't just beat—it lunges.

Time slows and it's like seconds drift into minutes until she nods. It's so small, if you weren't looking for it, you'd definitely miss it. But I'm looking. I've always been looking. She looks over the balcony edge, and her side silhouette could bring me to my knees.

I free one of my hands and use a finger to gently put it under her chin, pulling her focus back to me, tipping her face up to mine.

"Do you want me to kiss you?"

Only inches separate us. I swear I can feel the beat of her racing heart, or maybe it's mine. She's looking at me like there's something she has to discover, lifting corners and checking behind things. Hunting for the truth that maybe we've *both* been dodging. She must find what she's looking for because a smirk pulls at one corner of her lips, and she's pressing into me.

Fuck. She's going to kiss me.

Blair's lips are a moment away, a place I've wanted to go since I met her.

"Hey," Someone rounds the corner. At the sound of the voice, the feel of the steps, we both step away from each other. "Zack said I had to bring one of these out." A teammate holds up an espresso martini. "He said he got new coffee beans for Blair to try."

The universe is conspiring against me.

Her hand easily slips from mine like she's afraid to leave evidence behind.

"Thanks," she says, accepting the drink with a smile that is nowhere close to what she was just giving me. Her cheeks are flushed—guilty or frustrated or both. Mine too.

The guy doesn't notice a thing. He leaves. The air stays thick.

Blair ducks her head, breathing out a shaky laugh. "Of course."

I can't take my eyes off her mouth—the almost of it all.

"We should...go back in," she says, but her voice wavers like she's not sure she means it.

I nod, because if I speak, it'll be her name and a plea.

We step inside. Music swallows us. People pull her away. She glances over her shoulder, and the look says: Later. Please let there be a later.

I'm left standing there, heart still leaning toward her like we never stepped apart —knowing one more second alone and I would've finally tasted her.

The Game Day Tribune

COSMOS HOLD OFF DUCKS, CONTINUE TO REDEFINE NFL SPECIAL TEAMS PLAY

UPSTATE, N.Y.–The Upstate Cosmos beat the Detroit Ducks 26-14 on Sunday afternoon, riding a now-signature mix of gutsy play-calling, power runs, and a little bit of chaos.

For the third week in a row, the Cosmos leaned on an aggressive, field-goal-optional approach–and once again, it worked.

They went 2-for-4 on two-point conversions this time; not quite the clean sweep they pulled off against Seattle, but enough to keep control.

Blair Miller, in just her third game as the first woman ever on an NFL roster, added two more extra points to her total. She also attempted herå first career field goal–a 35-yarder late in the fourth quarter. The ball had distance but drifted wide right.

"I told her before the game, 'They're gonna let you try one. Be ready,'" said injured kicker Benny White, who watched from a suite with friends and family. "She was ready. That's all you can ask. She's got nerves I haven't seen in this league in a long time."

Miller's jersey remains the best seller in the league for another week.

White, sidelined indefinitely with a femur and tibia injury, has remained a vocal supporter of Miller. He stood for the kick, clapped when it missed, and cheered her on from the suite.

Miller was mobbed after her second extra point in the fourth—not because it was desperately needed, but because her teammates clearly want her to win as badly as the scoreboard does.

The Cosmos are on a three game winning streak with one field goal attempt and the same amount of misses. Their offense seems to thrive in unconventional situations, while their kicker is rewriting league history every week. And their special teams unit, once the question mark of the preseason, has become the heartbeat of one of the most unlikely starts in the NFL this year.

The Cosmos are headed to Illinois for an away game versus the Chicago Cougars next week.

Eleven

Blair

"WHAT DO YOU MEAN there's a mob outside the studio?" I ask Tiffany. I'm trying to get situated in my office, waiting for the familiarity and comfort to wash over me, but that's impossible when you've been putting out fires for the last two days.

Not literal fires, but things that pull me from my to-do list—the one I love to complete—and deal with things like a glitch in our booking system which basically doubled the capacity for a yoga class. Or a typo in the schedule which had twenty eight people showing up for a 9 PM yoga class that was meant for the morning.

Then there's the paparazzi encounters—more negative than previous. It's uncomfortable for our members, and my staff, to be bombarded by camera flashes while you're trying to get to and from a workout.

I'm thankful for everyone's grace and understanding. Staff, gym members, the police officer who I called when I was nervous about someone with a camera lurking by our staff entrance. Meanwhile, it feels like my body is in a vice, the air around me too heavy to even take a deep breath. This is my fault—it's me they're trying to see or maybe someone famous coming to work out—and that means I've tried taking on more than usual. Which is quite the choice, considering I've never had less time.

It's like something horrible is about to happen—I can feel the tide about to shift. There's nothing like waiting for the wave that's going to demolish everything in its path. And this place, which is so much of me, means everything.

Tiffany shifts her weight in the doorway, "Exactly what it sounds like. There's a line of people who are trying to come in. Some have gym bags, like they want to drop in, and some are saying they just want to buy merch."

"Are any of them members?"

"I don't think so. The members are coming in and using their cards to unlock the front. Security hasn't had any issues."

The entry system is new. It was necessary when we got the influx of new signups and it's honestly a great way to make sure the gym doesn't have too many people at once—I don't need any issues with the fire marshal. This was an upgrade I was looking to make in the next two years but didn't have the funds to complete it. Now, my original plan didn't include a security guard, but it was recommended with the increase in traffic and popularity.

"Let's make sure that security is doing okay and have them make an announcement."

"What's the announcement?" Tiffany asks when I don't immediately offer it up.

Rubbing my temples with my hands, I go into problem solving mode. Honestly, it's where it feels like I've been living lately. My brain gets all murky; one second it's fixated on how I wish I looked different in a football uniform, then it's on the calls and texts I'm behind on, before it jumps to something else.

The last few days there have been some honorable mentions—the missed field goal and the almost kiss with Tyson. It's like I don't have enough time or mental energy to think through these things. So, I get a third of the way in, trying to sort it out, and then we're on to the next.

The field goal was supposed to be no pressure—give me a challenge—but since I missed it, there's been this pit in my stomach that refuses to close. It's like I'm teetering on the edge and about to fall in at any moment. Coach clapped me on the shoulder and my teammates told me good job. They called out the positives: you had the leg, you were so close, you'll make it next time.

Being able to kick a field goal is key to every team's game plan. The Cosmos are at a disadvantage with someone who can only come in for extra points—and even then, it's still kind of a question mark. I haven't missed yet, but I have only had a few opportunities. Everyone said it was fine that I missed the attempt, and people even cheered on my miss, but it was like a punch to the gut.

"Blair?" Tiffany interrupts my thoughts.

"Sorry. Okay, here's what we'll do. Give everyone a business card, have them sign up for the newsletter, and we'll make changes to our schedule in the next few weeks. We'll add a designated time to shop for merch plus an additional drop in time for non-members."

"Wait. That's brilliant," She lifts her hands and rests them on her cheeks. "Should we get merch?"

I laugh because she's right. The only things we have are a logo T-shirt, stickers, and a water bottle. Again, this is something I wanted to expand on when I had the time and funds. Guess there's no time like the present. "Yes. I'll work on it."

Another item to add to the never-ending to-do list.

"Anything I can help you with?" Tiffany asks.

"I'm sure but I don't even know where to start right now. Let's go take care of the mob and we'll go from there. Okay?"

My phone buzzes on my desk.

Tyson: want to do takeout tonight?

Tyson: can give you the rundown on the away game schedule

I flip the phone over, as if Tyson can see me through the screen. He's another thing my brain has been running through, ever since the Halloween party. Ever since we almost kissed.

The way he looked at me... This time, there was no second guessing. His blue eyes were like waters I could happily drown in. And the disappointment that crashed into me when we were interrupted. The balcony felt like a movie, all of the almosts coming to a tipping point, and I was eager to see what was coming next. Instead, Zack's thoughtfulness and remembering my love for coffee was like someone turning the lights on in the theater just as the big reveal was to hit the screen.

Me: as long as you're cool with a late dinner

Me: I'm here until 8:30 tonight

Tyson: see you then

The nerves dance to the top of my skin, flushing it pink—I can feel the warmth and start to fan myself with a promotional postcard on my desk.

I force a slow breath and try to shut out the noise beyond my office walls. My heart is sprinting, not from fear but... anticipation? Hope? It's wild to think that all this time I convinced myself what I felt for Tyson was ridiculous. Safe to ignore when he was a few states away, tucked neatly into the part of my life labeled *off-limits*.

But now he's here. And he's looking at me like I'm not just in the background anymore. Like he sees me.

And when he leaned in—God, I swear he was going to kiss me. Not a friendly, 'whoops, we were too close' kiss. A real one. The kind you feel everywhere. The kind you don't imagine unless the other person wants it, too.

Maybe I wasn't the only one holding on to something invisible between us. Maybe that shift I kept secretly waiting for... wasn't wishful thinking after all. Maybe it's been there, quietly building, long before tonight.

I think back to one night in the library our junior year, when it was just the two of us utilizing those late night hours offered at the end of a term.

The whole campus seemed to be breathing in its sleep, the air thick with the smell of old books and the coffee left to cool beside my notebook. It started out as a group of us, but as everyone left, one by one, Tyson stayed. He should be in bed, resting for morning practice, yet here he was, slouched across from me, head buried in a book for a class I knew he had an A in.

The fluorescent lights buzzed overhead, and every turn of a page seems to echoes. My eyes burned from reading, matching the ache in my shoulders, and when a chill crept in from the window, I shivered. Tyson's eyes flicked up from the textbook and without a word, he slid his hoodie across the table, its fabric warm and faintly scented like him. Our fingers brushed as I took it—his touch lingered just a second too long, the kind of second that makes the world hold its breath.

Right then, the way he looked at me isn't casual. It wasn't friendly. It was heavy, like gravity itself had shifted between us. His gaze held mine, steady and unflinching, and for a heartbeat I could feel the air swirling around us, like something inevitable was about to break open.

I could almost hear the soft scrape of his chair, imagined him leaning across the table, his breath mingling with mine. My pulse drummed in my ears, and I felt ready—ready to close the distance, to find out what that look meant. But then he blinked, the tension breaking like a wave on the shore. He smiled that small, disarming smile of his—the one that always made it hard to be angry at him—and looked back down at his open book. The moment passed quietly, like the whisper of a page turning. No kiss. No confession. Just the ghost of what could have been lingering in the air between us in an empty library.

And that's the thing—Tyson has always been that guy. Thoughtful, steady, someone who makes everyone feel seen. I told myself I wasn't special. That I imagined it.

But now, when I think back to that night, I can't ignore the truth that maybe he pulled back because he was scared, too. Maybe he felt it and didn't know what to do with it. Maybe we've been running from the same thing–afraid to cross the line.

I always thought I wasn't what he wanted... the type of woman he'd see himself with. Just one of the guys and nothing more.

But at the party? The way he looked at me—like he was finally ready to close that space between us—it was like he was about to meet me halfway.

And suddenly, I'm done pretending there's nothing there. The grin painting my lips tells me everything I need to know about my plan for tonight. Sometimes, you have to put yourself out there to get the answers you need.

THE DIGITAL CLOCK BLINKS at me: 8:36 pm. I've been here since 7 AM and there's still work I could do, but there's somewhere else I have to be. My stomach flips at the realization—I'd rather be with Tyson than be here.

Now that's really saying something.

Embers and Ashes is my everything—my proudest accomplishment—and the place I feel most myself. It's an odd occurrence if I'm not here for at least a few hours each day... even If I'm not teaching a class or scheduled to work. It's hard to pull myself away, quit knocking things off the to-do list.

But tonight? It's Tyson.

I'm walking out the door, security making sure I safely get to my car, when my phone buzzes. When I'm in my car and the doors are locked, I pull out my phone. There's a missed call from a number I don't know. Probably spam.

Before I can text Ty, letting him know I'm on my way, the number comes through again. I don't know what it is but something tells me to answer it.

"Hello?" I wait for the expected awkward silence and click of a telemarketer.

Instead, I'm met with a voice I didn't expect. But even after all these years I'd know it in my bones.

"Hey, little bee."

My dad.

Twelve

Blair

"Wʜᴀᴛ ᴅɪᴅ ʏᴏᴜ ᴊᴜsᴛ say?"

The voice on the other end crackles with a laugh, worn in and one I haven't heard in almost twenty years. "You remembered. I knew you would."

My hands are clammy enough I feel like the phone could slip right out of my hand.

"Mitchell, why are you calling me?"

"Mitchell? First naming me, huh? "

"Well, calling you dad feels like a crime, so."

There's that laugh again. He seems so unbothered. Not like he's calling his only daughter for the first time in twenty years. Anger coils, deep in my belly, bringing tears to my eyes.

"You were always the quick one. How are you, little bee?"

I look around, trying to find the camera or something designed to capture my reaction, because this has to be a bit. Nothing else makes sense. I don't even know how he'd have my phone number.

"What do you want?"

"What, a father can't call up his kids every now and again?"

My words are sharp and quick, "They can but you're not really a father, now are you?" The other line is quiet besides for some background noise—maybe a TV or the radio. "Are you sick or something?" I go to the only thing I can fathom that would have this man—this stranger—call me.

"No, I'm not sick. Everything's fine."

I let silence fill the space between us and it's as if a rope is being pulled taut. There's a flame low enough not to catch it all at once, but the braids are starting to fray.

Tears slide down my face. They're full of anger and questions and hurt I never got to express to him.

"I saw you've been playing in the NFL." His voice is enthusiastic and it's like skinning your knee running to get ice cream on the first day of summer. Something that should be so fun and exciting but then it's ruined.

"Yes."

"That's pretty cool. I've been able to tell my buddies that that's my girl out there. Don't get to see you buzz around, like I did at your soccer games, but it's still something."

My girl. The words feel like they're burning my skin—leaving red marks and blisters. How is this happening? How could the man who was supposed to look after me, after us, get up and leave without anything more than a card on my eighteenth birthday? And then he calls acting like nothing has happened.

"You shouldn't lie to your friends like that. I haven't been your girl for a long time, Mitchell." It's as if the words are programmed and I don't know where they're coming from. I am borderline having an out of body experience.

"You'll always be my girl." His voice is quiet, almost hard to hear.

I breathe in, filling my lungs, and sigh the breath out. "It's sad that you think that. You really shouldn't. People who leave their families, never to be heard from again, don't get to do that." The way my voice cracks at the end of the sentence hits me hard. I don't want him to hear me cry, to know that he impacted me like this.

Keep it together. You can have a meltdown once you hang up. I barter with myself, willing my body to hold it in.

"I'm going to be over that way in a few weeks. Wondered if you got tickets for games or anything like that. I'd love to come see you play."

There it is.

"Are you fucking for real right now? Tell me you didn't call to ask me for tickets to a football game?" The silence on the other end tells me everything I need to know. The rage that was coiling is ready to spring and I can feel it releasing, taking me with it. "You never called when my high school soccer team went to state finals, two years in a row, or when I was the leading scorer of my college team and we made it to the post season. Or when I graduated—high school or college. Or when I opened my own business. You. Never. Called."

"I know, and…" The pause he lets drag amplifies my hurt. Hurt fueled by rage. "I'm sorry about that." His voice is level, steady—like the dad I wished he would've been. If I didn't know exactly what kind of person he was, maybe I'd have a chance to believe in his apology.

But I do, so I don't.

"Don't be. I did just fine without you." My eyes gaze outside the window, a few flurries blowing in the chilled November air. "If you're actually sorry, you won't call me again. Bye, Mitchell."

I end the call before he can say another word. My chest heaves with shallow breaths, the air rushed and too loud. It's like my ribcage grows by the breath, getting too big for my skin to fit over it. I try to catch my breath but my ears are filled with pounding and it's distracting. My heart. Too fast. Too much.

This is all too much.

I place one hand on my belly and the other on my chest. I'm grasping at anything to try and level myself. Trying to feel my breathing, the beat of my heart, whatever I can to bring myself back down.

It doesn't feel like it's working, so I shut my eyes, tears streaming down my cheeks, and put my head in my hands. The sound that fills the inside of my car catches me off guard—it's strangled and painful. I look in the rear view mirror and realize it's me. That sound came from me.

Part of me always wondered what would happen if my dad came back around. In my head, he always had this hefty apology; one with remorse and the kind you can feel the pain singe the edges. He tells us why he had to leave and it makes at least a little sense. He begs to have a conversation, anything we'd be willing to give him.

With that phone call, he stole something from me. Something I didn't know was up for grabs.

Hope. That's what he stole. Hope that he'd try to make the horrible thing he did right. Hope that he'd find a way to redeem the first man I was supposed to love. The realization would bring me to my knees if I wasn't already crumpled in this car.

I need to get out of here. I put the keys in the ignition, feel the engine turn over, and let muscle memory take me home. The roads are practically empty and I use all the mental capacity I have to be a responsible driver.

I grip the steering wheel, letting my knuckles turn white, like the few snowflakes trying to stick. Even though I try to breathe through it, and keep the tears at bay, I'm unsuccessful. Tears continue to fall, steady and heavy, bringing with it all the things I thought were behind me when it came to this man—the piece of the puzzle that never resurfaced.

And then it hits me, the thought I've run from for a long time...

The man meant to care for me didn't love me enough to stay. So why would anyone else?

Thirteen

Tyson

COACH WOULD BE PISSED if he knew I drank too much bourbon last night and am now acting like I'm not hungover as I walk on the team plane. But what he doesn't know won't hurt him.

Blair didn't show up. She didn't call and when I tried calling her, she sent me to voicemail, only to text me saying she was too tired and lost track of time. I sat and stared at cold takeout, racking my brain for what it meant, and when I thought I had a handle on it, I was already pouring bourbon for dinner.

I've seen Blair when she's had three hours of sleep in two days but even then she didn't want to cancel plans. We've been to the movies when she's fallen asleep in the middle due to soccer practice and studying kicking her ass, plus her waiting for me to get out of night class, so we could see something together.

But last night was different.

Fuck, it stung.

I get settled in my seat and try to think of something else. Football is my job and no matter how shitty I feel, I owe it to my team, coaches, and fans, to separate all that be ready to work.

Even when I see her walk on to the plane wearing a Cosmos hat. I think she'll look for me, maybe even want to take an empty seat in my row. Instead, she slides into the first empty row she sees, grabbing a window seat.

I wonder if she's nervous. Excited. This is the first time she's traveling with the team and it feels weird to not know. To not be part of it.

The last thing I ever wanted to do was make her uncomfortable or change things. Fuck, that's really what I didn't want. It felt like everything I wanted was in reach. I could almost see a future I've wanted for so long—me and Blair together. So close I could almost taste it... feel her lips on mine.

And she didn't even show up. Maybe getting interrupted let her figure out what she really wanted. From here, it doesn't look like that's me, and that fucking hurts.

WE'RE WINNING THIS GAME but we sure of hell don't deserve it. In the first half, our quarterback threw two interceptions—both returned for a touchdown—and our special teams fumbled a punt return, giving the ball back to them at the seven yard line.

It's the start of the third quarter and Tripp Owens just caught a touchdown pass and we're ahead by a single point. Lining up for the extra point, the cheers are almost deafening—the norm since Blair has been part of the team. It's amazing how excited everyone gets when she steps on the field.

No matter what's going on between us, she will always be one of my favorite people, and seeing her do this will never get old.

I hear the kick of the ball and then see it go wide right. She missed. Her first miss. I watch her jog off the field, teammates tapping her helmet and shoulder in support.

As we go on defense, I keep trying to catch her eyes but she doesn't even take her helmet off. She keeps her chin down, motion tight. Zack and Coach Dylan crowd around her with the tablet, showing her the kick, trying to break down what went wrong. I know that look—she's barely hearing a word of it. She's somewhere else, locked up in her own head, beating herself up.

My ankle throbs—I tweaked it early in the game. I keep moving it, shifting my weight back and forth, not pushing the tape job too far but not letting the muscles get cold. I know my leg is compensating, the tightness pulling on my hamstrings and quads. I can't think about it for too long because it's not just the leg, it's my whole body.

I look around and find a few Cosmos fans in the first rows behind us—common for away games. There's a dad holding a little girl, wearing a Zack Andersen jersey, and an older boy with his mom, wearing a generic Cosmos hoodie. The little boy catches me looking and he waves, his eyes lighting up in the way he knows I see him. I wave back and it's like part of me is splitting from itself.

Sometimes, playing football is like walking willingly into a car crash. The promise of the big hits or stops was what kept me going when I first got into the league. Now, I'm not so sure. I wonder what it would be like where you go to work and you're not worried about breaking a bone, tearing a ligament, pulling a muscle, or putting your brain at risk.

I glance at Blair again. She's got her hands clasped tight between her knees, helmet still on, jaw locked like she's holding everything in. And yeah, it stings that she won't look at me. But I can tell this isn't just about a missed kick. Something shifted recently—off the field—and even if she won't say it, I can feel it in the way she keeps bracing against the world. I know I should be hurt, but mostly I just want to be let in. I want her to be okay.

This game? The team aspect? I love it. But it's moments like this when I feel it shifting into past tense—something I loved and was proud to be part of.

Wondering about what comes next.

Fourteen

Blair

I wasn't thinking about football. The kick. The team. The score. None of it. I was on a completely different planet and it showed.

Now, I'm still not thinking about it.

I can't believe my dad called me the way he did.

I can't believe I stood Tyson up.

I can't believe I can't shake this.

It feels like my world is spinning too fast for me to put my shoes on, I can't even tie them, but someone is asking me to run a marathon. Everything is a blur and my arms are swinging about, trying to grab something to slow it down.

When I ended the call with my dad last night, I got in my car and drove. I didn't know where I was going, but I rolled the windows down and let the air freeze me out. It was an hour one way before turning back around on the expressway and heading home.

The only sounds in the car were the wind from the open windows and the chatter of my teeth. I didn't know I was crying until my cheeks started to burn.

When I got back to my place, I stayed in my car. Unable to move. Unable to really do anything. My phone sat in my hand, hovering over names to call. Tyson. My mom. My brothers. Maggie. I didn't have it in me to do anything.

And that was like throwing dry brush into the fire. Like the anxiety and indecision kept sharpening the knife that was at my throat.

I didn't think a phone call from the man who left us behind would ever impact me like this. Always thought I was above it–I really didn't miss or need him. Whenever people gave me that look on Father's Day, when they knew I didn't have a relationship with that man, I'd reassure them that it was a non-issue.

Don't feel sorry for me.

Now, here I am, feeling even more sorry for myself than I thought possible.

I hate that he's still taking things from me.

I'm supposed to be stronger than this.

With no idea how long I was in the car, I made my way to my place and then just sat on my kitchen floor. And then, it was four in the morning–only a few hours until I needed to get on the team plane for my first away game.

This morning, after two hours of sleep, I woke up in a panic over Tyson. I knew he'd understand... he always did. But it felt like things had finally lined up–our planets finally in the same orbit–and it was something else I was grasping at, unsuccessfully.

I opened my messages and froze when I saw all the unread notifications. Maggie. Tyson. Coach Dylan. Zack. Benny. Bella. Tiffany. My brothers. This is what set off the first panic attack. How could this much happen in just a few hours? How could they all need something from me?

The idea of doing anything had me frozen as the room started to spin and my vision started to become a pin point.

Breathe in. Hold for four. Out.

Again.

Again.

Again.

I'm back there again. Running through it, start to finish. The phone call. The driving. The wallowing. The game. The miss. The hurt.

I'm sitting in the small women's locker room and even though the team won, it doesn't feel like it. Catching a glance of myself shows the worst posture I've ever had: shoulders slumped, belly showing over my leggings. My finger pokes the skin. I know there's muscle underneath it but the grim reaper that is my confidence and body dysmorphia show up.

Like the old friend you wish would lose your number.

Anger starts to bubble as I stand, looking at my silhouette in the mirror. My brain does that awful thing where it takes reality and warps it, stretching every flaw like it's under a carnival mirror spotlight. The shape of my stomach. The way my thighs press together. The soft line under my sports bra that wouldn't be there if I were truly strong enough, disciplined enough, worthy enough.

Tears chase each other as the seconds stretch into minutes. The negative thoughts in my head are louder than any scoreboard. Louder than any compliment I've ever gotten. Louder than the part of me that knows I'm more than this surface level hate.

A knock sounds from the hall—voices getting closer. I wipe my eyes fast, but the redness stays.

"Blair? You ready?" Zack asks.

Turning from the mirror, trying to leave the loathing behind, I grab my bags and do my best to compose myself. When he sees me, the bright demeanor he wears like a proud badge drops and his brows press together.

"It was one kick. Please don't beat yourself up like this." His arm wraps around my shoulder, pulling me into him. The softness of his voice. The concern on his face.

It's all I need to push myself off the edge I've been teetering on and completely fall apart.

Fifteen

Tyson

Our team dinner is at the hotel restaurant and the vibes are nowhere to be found. Today ended with a notch in the win column but it doesn't necessarily feel like it. There were some things that went our way but I wouldn't say we were the better team or we outplayed them.

My eyes keep watching the door, scanning the corners, looking for Blair. Maybe she's back at the room? Pulling my phone out of my pocket, my stomach drops when I see no messages.

Fuck. We're in the same hotel—we would've killed for this—but it's all messy. This isn't how it's supposed to be. She's my best friend but there's this crater between the two of us—it's like both of us are afraid to cross.

I'm walking toward the elevator when I see someone pacing out of the corner of my eye. Blair. She's on the phone and is walking the short distance, back and forth, between hallway walls. From here, I can see her shoulders shake as she turns away from me. She's crying.

And something pulls me towards the hallway. I have to stop myself from jogging over to her, wrapping her up in my arms, and let her feel whatever she's feeling, but not feel it alone. The pull is jarring, like something deep in my bones, and the only thing I can do is keep my feet firmly planted on the too-shiny hotel tile.

She puts a hand through her hair, pulling it at the end, like her fingers need something to do. Blair shows her face, just for a second, and I can see her cheeks are crimson—the way they turn when she's either really pissed off or has been crying.

Before I can make a decision, she pulls the phone from her face and looks up. Finding me. *You idiot,* my brain teases, *now what the fuck do I do? Do I go to her? Turn and walk back to the restaurant? Wave?* I hear people getting off the elevator and that's what I decide. Moving to the elevator, I feel Blair behind me. Hitting the button, the doors open and I step in. Fixating on the floor, tan tiles with gold speckles, I hold my breath when she steps in.

Blair wipes her face with the backs of her hands as she leans her back on the opposite corner of mine. She sniffles in a way that she's trying to not make a sound and it hurts me... her trying to make herself small even when it's just the two of us.

Fuck. I don't want that.

The elevator slowly climbs the floors and I break the silence. "Do you want to talk about it?"

Blair sniffles, "There's nothing to talk about. I'm in the best mood," she tries to joke, and keeps looking forward.

"Blair." Her name comes off my lips like I'm pleading with her to let me in.

Her lips are pressed together in the thinnest line, and she looks up at the ceiling, like she's bargaining with the tears.

"I can't. Really. I can't." Her voice gets quieter with each word.

She bites her lip, looking at me, saying nothing else. I nod, not wanting to push her.

"I really am fine. Just need to get some sleep," Blair repeats like she's trying to reassure herself.

I know this version of her. The one who would rather suffer and do any-thing besides ask for help, lean on someone else. She doesn't like seeming soft, or maybe she views it as weak, even though there's no way anyone could ever call her that. Typically, the way I've gotten her out of this is a distraction. A random fact. A weird 'would you rather.' Challenge her to compete against me doing something menial and ridiculous—like who can eat a bowl of marshmallows the fastest, or who could chug a drink first, or who could hold a plank the longest.

I can't think of anything besides the one thing I've been dying to do. Ever since I've met her. Ever since I've learned what kind of person she is—brave, bright, with a competitive streak that's tough to beat. The elevator continues to rise toward the top floors, where the team is staying, and it's only the two of us.

The elevator makes no stops and I'm running out of time.

"Hey," I say, stepping closer to her, grabbing her arm to turn her towards me.

She looks up at me and I can't stop staring at her lips, the mouth that I know has a sharp retort waiting for me. And before that retort can hit me, or the doors open, I pull her close to me.

We're a breath apart when her coffee colored eyes, framed by her thick lashes, look to my lips. Before anything can ruin this, I lean in.

And I kiss her.

Sixteen

Blair

Tyson is kissing me.

His lips find mine and it catches me off guard. I was almost expecting him to fight me on what was wrong, but he didn't. Instead, he put his lips to mine and held me up in a way I didn't expect.

The kiss is soft but claiming—his lips pressing into me and his hand finding my jawline then resting underneath my chin. Tyson's lips are full on mine as his tongue lightly sweeps over my bottom lip, looking for more. I open and let him taste me. When the kiss is deeper, he moans into me. That sound. That reaction? It's everything I've dreamt of, held out for, hoped would happen. My lips turn up, smirking into his kiss.

This kiss breaks and chips at some of the stone that feels like it has wrapped around me over the last twenty-four hours.

His other hand finds my cheek before putting both of his hands in my hair, his fingers scratching at my scalp before resting at the nape of my neck. His hands are massive so his thumbs rest on the column of my neck and I can feel the flames start to simmer in my low belly.

I want him. I need him. Maybe this is supposed to be where we ended up all along?

I take a step closer, my chest almost flush with his, as I tip up, his height impressive and so fucking attractive right now. When I go to put a hand in his floppy hair, the elevator stops.

We're apart like there's a rope around our waists, pulling as to our separate corner as the doors open. A few of our teammates, luckily with their backs to us, are chatting and waiting for the elevator.

This is my floor—most of the team is spread out between three of them—so I give Tyson one last look before stepping off.

Looks like the guys getting on the elevator are about to go out, so I say, "Have fun tonight," with a little wave, as I breeze past them down the corridor.

Tyson's eyes? I can feel them on me. Up until the sound of doors closing. It feels like I'm running in the opposite direction. Instead, I wish I was going to his room, meeting him there, picking up where we left off. But even I know it's too risky.

I tap the room key to the door and step inside, immediately turning the heat down on the thermostat because my skin is flushed pink, already hot. I sit at the end of the bed, mouth open, trying to think about what just happened. First, I'm on the phone with Jay, telling him about the phone call from our dad, and next, Tyson is kissing me in the elevator. And I was kissing him back.

Walking into the bathroom, I stand in front of the mirror. My cheeks are red; if you look closely you can see the trails from where the tears fell. Putting a finger to my lips, a contrast to what Tyson's mouth felt like, brings a smile to my lips.

Messy. That's what I feel like. There's so much to unpack and it's like I don't have the time or space to figure anything out. Including the pain and anger from my brothers when I told them. Tyson kissing me. The realization of how much I wanted him to cross that line.

What does this mean? The thought hits me like a punch to the gut, the kind when you're playing with your older brothers and they forget you're their little sister–hitting you a little too hard. Surprising and a bit confusing. Well, I want to tell him about my dad. I almost did but the words were trapped. I couldn't. The only person I've told, besides my brothers, was Zack—not even Mags. And that's because he watched me burst into tears after the game. He was so kind, then told me a lovely story about his own family, blended and complicated but full of love. It was like the universe put that story in front of me on a day where it would sting the most.

I was ugly crying and Zack was convinced I was having a breakdown. The pressure of being on the team catching up with me and it was too much to handle. He had this whole scenario built out, and I had to hand it to him, because that was some significance and elite overthinking. So, to ease his mind, and also buy myself some time for getting on the bus back to the hotel, I told him. I gave him the high level version of the man who left, never called or returned, until he needed something from me.

Zack hugged me, holding on the way an old friend does. He patted my back and swayed me back and forth, telling me how sorry he was. I believed him. And it almost made it hurt worse. I've known Zack for a couple of weeks and the way he acted when I told him, the pain filling his eyes and his energy dipping down to meet me—the compassion was overwhelming. It really solidified how awful it was of my dad to do this. At first, it was something only I was dealing with, and then Zack just proved me right. Cathartic and like one of the deepest cuts I've felt in my life.

Honestly? I wanted to tell Tyson in the elevator. I wanted to spill my guts and have us go somewhere so I could tell him everything. We've never had secrets or anything like this between us, that I know of, and I need the support. My brothers love me and they were obviously on my side, but they have their own pain and rage to sort through. I need someone like Ty.

But then he was kissing me and it felt like my world was flipping... like I was at the top of the rollercoaster and it finally sped down the dip of the track. My hand presses to my belly, remembering the feeling of the drop, the one I've wanted for longer than I care to admit.

My phone buzzes.

Tyson

> you have no idea how long I've wanted to do that

Me

> really?

> really

> good night, blair

Turning on the water of the shower, I realize something.

I don't want to be just friends with Ty. I can't even imagine it.

Now that the line is crossed, I need to figure out what we do to move forward.

The Game Day Tribune

COSMOS SURVIVE IN CHICAGO, HEAD INTO BYE WEEK WITH MOMENTUM AND QUESTIONS

CHICAGO, IL–The Upstate Cosmos eked out a 26-24 win over the Chicago Cougars on Sunday afternoon, keeping their win streak alive despite a shakier outing than weeks past–particularly on special teams.

Rookie kicker Blair Miller, whose rise has been one of the most talked-about storylines of the season, went just 2 for 4 on extra point attempts. Her timing looked off, her plant foot slipped once, and yet the crowd cheered her on anyway–not mockingly, but with a kind of tentative encouragement usually reserved for underdogs and the players that have that kind of spark surrounding them.

While Miller was inconsistent, the Cosmos didn't attempt a 2-point conversion after scoring any of their four touchdowns. The Cougars are a tough defense to crack when it comes to getting two after scoring a touchdown; maybe that's why the Cosmos didn't even attempt? Or maybe, it's the coaching staff trying to get Miller as many in-game snaps as possible.

The Game Day Tribune

The Cougars nearly staged a comeback in the final two minutes, but an interception by linebacker Trey Caldwell sealed the win.

Now 4-0 since Miller joined the roster, the Cosmos remain one of the league's most unconventional teams—gritty, chaotic, and proud of it. But the spark that once felt electric around Miller has dimmed slightly, or maybe just settled into something more human.

With a bye week ahead and Thanksgiving looming, the Cosmos get a moment to breathe—and maybe recalibrate—before their next test at home versus the Dallas Lone Stars.

Seventeen

Tyson

I KISSED BLAIR. I fucking did it. She didn't push me away or tell me to stop—she put herself into it. My cheeks sting because I'm that annoying bastard who's been smiling like a kid on his birthday any time I've been thinking about it. And let's be for real, it's been difficult to think about anything else.

Sliding into my seat, row 27 and by the window, I get settled for the flight. My stomach flips thinking about the one practice we'll have before heading into the bye week, which couldn't come at a better time. Since we're playing on Thanksgiving, the coaching staff changes up the schedule so we can all have as much time away from the facility as possible. We have some workouts planned, but you do them wherever you are.

I can't wait to spend a few days with Blair, out of the city. Ever since I met her in college, she's always come to my family Thanksgiving. It's hard not to remember the first time I asked her to come home with me.

"You running like that because you're about to have a few days off? Or did that treadmill commit a crime?" I ask as Blair pounds her feet as she damn near sprints next to me. Ever since I met her, we've been studying together or working out when we're not at practice.

She looks down at the time and when she hits a specific number, she removes some of the speed and slows down to a walk next to me. "No days off for me. I've got no Thanksgiving plans."

Blair gave me the rundown on her family, mentioning her mom and two older brothers, but while I always try to make it home to Michigan, I can't remember a time where she went home. Family is difficult or maybe it's hard to line up schedules?

"What do you mean you're staying here? It's Thanksgiving. Turkey, rolls, and pie? You love those pumpkin drinks from the café, how can you not like Thanksgiving?!"

Her eyes, golden like the last of the autumn leaves clinging to the trees, stare ahead. "My family isn't big on the holidays. My dad left when I was twelve and after that it just became too much for my mom. I didn't push it. When I was in high school, we'd order pizza and watch old movies."

Pizza on Thanksgiving. Her shifty eyes look to me and the sad smile on her lips has my heart squeezing in my chest. I know every family isn't like mine but it's so difficult to imagine that for someone like her. She's close with her brothers and typically talks about home like she misses it. But it's got to be much more complicated than that. I'm sort of kicking myself for assuming she'd have this massive holiday at home, just because my parents don't know how to chill out when we're together.

"Are your brothers going to be around or are you really just planning on staying in the dorms?"

"No, they've got girlfriends and other things to get to. Just me this year. It's no big deal." The line that falls out of her mouth is one she's said more times than anyone should.

I stop the treadmill, my cool down walk just about finished, and look out the window. Snow is starting to fall, flakes thick and gorgeous when you're safely inside. I can't imagine Blair in her tiny dorm room while I'm back at home with the bustle and comfort of being with family. It will only be a two-day trip—that's the max Coach could allow this season based on the football schedule—but it's better than nothing.

What if you invited her? The thought runs through my brain but like it's carrying a little bag full of doubt and fear. What if she thinks it's weird? Too much? What if she's looking forward to time away from me? Twelve—that's when her dad left. She probably hasn't had a full holiday, like I'm used to, in that long.

And that's the tipping point.

"Why don't you come home with me?" I ask as Blair continues to walk on the treadmill, her cheeks red from the work.

"You don't have to do that, Ty." She wags her finger and only looks at me for a moment.

"I know I don't have to, I want to. Plus, if my parents find out that I left you here like this? I'll be in trouble."

She stops her treadmill and turns to look at me, putting a hand on her hip and shifting the weight. "You want me to fly home with you? Crash your Thanksgiving?" She scrunches her forehead in the way she does when she's trying to make sense of something. It's fucking adorable.

"Yes. I'm only going to be there for two days, practice and stuff, but we have lots of space and my mom would love to meet you."

She tilts her head, letting out a quick breath, "Your mom knows about me?"

Fuck. Is that too much? Have I crossed into creeper territory?

"Of course she does. She knows about all my friends." I tell the little white lie. Well, actually it's not a lie. It's just that I've only had time for football and Blair. There really aren't any other friends to talk about. But I definitely don't tell her that.

"Are you sure? You really have the space?"

I do my best to reassure her, "Yes. More than enough space. My family would love it, I promise."

When she nods, agreeing to come, it's like a spark ignites in my chest. It's the first time I knew how much I wanted to bring her home. Even if we are just friends.

That Thanksgiving was one of my favorites. Blair walked in and fit like a piece of the puzzle we've been missing. My mom always joked about wanting girls but instead had two boys who turned out to be massive athletes who loved to be too rough. It was like Blair was exactly who she'd been waiting for.

Even now, almost ten years later, I remember thinking that, when I watched the two of them together. Blair had no idea how to bake, considering her mom never taught her, and she was enthralled with my mom while she was making her classic butterscotch apple pie.

We've had it every Thanksgiving since I can remember. Now, Blair makes it when she gets to my parents' house. Her own tradition with the family who loves her like she's one of us.

I can't wait to be home with Blair for another holiday in only a few days.

Just then, she gets on the plane, looking for a place to sit. She catches me looking at her, and gives a tip of her chin, and a small smile. Only for me.

"Do you mind if I sit?" Zack says, while putting his bag in the overhead bin.

"Not at all," I reply and Zack sits in the aisle row, leaving the middle seat open, the right move.

Once he's buckled in and ready for takeoff, he looks at me and asks, "You and Blair, you've really been friends since college? Like good friends?"

I nod. "Yeah, I met her my sophomore year. We were both student athletes and sort of clicked."

"I'm jealous. I don't have any friends like that. Especially not someone like Blair. She's fucking cool. I keep telling Emilie we have to get together, so she can meet her. Think the three of them would get along?" His voice climbs the way it does when he's planning something he's excited about.

By the three of them, I know he means Blair, Emilie, and Willow. Emilie is Zack's wife and she works for Willow—she started as her assistant but now has a pretty high-up job at Willow's music label. I know that if Blair had the opportunity to meet Willow, she'd lose her shit—that's one of her all-time favorite musicians. Everything I've learned about Willow, I've learned from Blair, up until being traded to the Cosmos where her fiancé Tripp Owens is on the team.

"She'd love it. Don't tell her I told you, but she's a bit obsessed with Willow," I confide in Zack as he claps his hands together, rubbing them like he's coming up with a mischievous plan.

He turns, scrunching his nose a bit and says, "You're like best friends, huh?" I nod and he continues, "I love that. It's like the universe needed you to have more time together this year or something."

He's right. I've thought a lot about how this season has panned out and it's not anything I expected or even thought possible. But here we are.

He coughs, leaning closer to me. "This stuff with her dad. I can't believe it. Hurts me to think about."

What? The look I give him must show my confusion.

"What guy calls his kid after almost twenty years like that?"

Her dad called? What is he talking about? First a wave of adrenaline hits me, wanting to know what he wanted, what he said. When did he call? I know in this moment, I need to keep my face from giving me away. I can't get into this with Zack.

I do everything I can to nod along and act like I totally get it.

"Yeah, I can't imagine," I say, turning to face the head seat in front of me, trying to end the conversation. Because honestly? I don't know what to fucking say.

"She's tough. That's for damn sure," Zack adds, in a way that shows the conversation is over.

I look out at the window, trying to get a grasp about what I just heard. Blair's dad called her? She told Zack. She didn't tell me. That's probably what she was crying about yesterday. I flat out asked her if she wanted to talk about it and she wouldn't.

But she told Zack.

Someone she just met?

The hurt catches me as soon as the plane starts to taxi down the runway. If I opened my mouth right now, I don't know if I could form words. My throat is tight and it feels like there's sand in my mouth... like you can't swallow past it. Quietly, I try to catch my breath. I look over and see that Zack is wearing an eye mask and is trying to sleep.

Breathe in.

Her dad called.

Breathe out.

Why didn't she tell me?

Breathe in.

What now?

Breathe out.

Who knows.

Eighteen

Blair

SEEING TYSON AT PRACTICE is what's keeping me going on limited amounts of caffeine this morning. I'm at Embers and Ashes, trying to wrap up a ridiculous amount of work before being off for a few days. Thanksgiving isn't until next week, but we're celebrating with Tyson's family early since the Cosmos have a Thanksgiving Day game next week.

I have a Thanksgiving Day game. Wow.

My brothers have shelled out some serious cash for tickets. Even though I would've paid for them, considering I fell into a bucket of money—at least for my standards—but they insisted.

I still think it's wild that NFL players don't get a ticket allotment for games. Yes, the staff will help them secure whatever they need, but everyone pays for them. Makes me wonder what Tyson paid for my birthday tickets. I shimmy my shoulders, shaking off the flush to my skin, and try to stay focused.

My to-do list is still too long, even though I got here at four in the morning, trying to catch up because of the away game trip this past weekend. There are so many things I want to oversee and take the lead on, but that makes it almost impossible. I know this isn't how successful businesses run, but it's like if I let up, even a little, the thing I've built will crumble down.

There's not a crack in the foundation, especially now—since I've joined the Cosmos, our membership have maxed out and we've sold out of every new piece of merch we've added to the shelves. I've hired more instructors and front office staff and still am more profitable than I've ever been.

I've been around the least I've ever managed since starting it—that part makes me feel a little sad. I know it's a testament to its success, but it's my favorite place to be, and since joining the Cosmos, I've spent very little time here.

Honestly? I think it's time to consider opening a second Embers and Ashes location. That's one of the reasons I've been holding onto the cash I got from the Cosmos. The goal wasn't to create an empire or anything like that, but I did want to offer up as many safe spaces for people as possible. My eyes water at the possibility.

I need to go back to therapy. The thought that I can't be all the way happy about my success is a massive red flag. There were nights I dreamt of getting the gym to this place, the one it's in right now, and I'm still not satisfied. Pair that with the unresolved trauma of parent abandonment and my body dysmorphia that's bubbled back up and I'm a therapist's dream!

Grabbing my phone, I set a reminder to call my therapist and make an appointment. I internally screech to myself when I see the time, needing to get to practice.

Today's practice was one for the books. I made five field goals, consecutively, ranging from five to eight yards further than an extra point. Each time the ball went through the uprights, every single person in the room was on another level—jumping up and down and cheering me on like I hit a game winner.

We're in the film room as the team discusses adjustments for the Thanksgiving game matchup, and I'm trying to find Tyson. Since we don't practice with the same groups, it's common that we do a bit of searching to find each other. But when the lights go down, and come back up after an hour of film, I still can't find him.

I decide to check with Coach Dylan—maybe he needed extra treatment or something—I know he tweaked his ankle during the game on Sunday. Down the corridor I walk to Coach's office, seeing the photos from all the key Cosmos moments thus far. Considering the Upstate Cosmos were an NFL expansion team and have only been in the league a few years, it's impressive to see what they've accomplished. Many NFL teams have never won a Super Bowl, but here are the Cosmos with two checks already in that column.

When I approach Coach's door, I hear the sounds of someone borderline yelling. I stop and wonder if I should turn around—I don't have an appointment or anything. Just when I'm about to pivot and head home, it's clear they're talking about me. Or *someone* is talking about me.

"This little PR stunt has run its course, don't you think? Women don't play in the NFL," the voice says; it's familiar but I don't know who it belongs to.

Coach Dylan's voice interrupts. "What is your issue? She has nothing to do with your client." His voice is barely raised but it's enough to raise my eyebrows.

"She's occupying my client's roster spot. I just need to know you're going to come when Benny is ready and there isn't going to be a murmur of keeping her on the roster."

I can't roll my eyes hard enough listening to Benny's slimy agent talk to Dylan about me. Part of me knows this isn't something meant for me to hear, but the other part of me is glued in place—there's absolutely no way I'm leaving.

Dylan says nothing; it feels like the office is frozen in time. Fuck, what if Oscar storms out and sees me? The rational part of my brain says, *Well, that's on him and he shouldn't be talking shit like this with the door open.*

"Oscar, get out of my office," Dylan snaps, the wheels of his chair moving on the floor the only sound. "And if you do this again, I'll make sure security doesn't even let you in next time."

There's another gap of silence and I use that to loudly walk outside, like I'm just now approaching the office and not like I was eavesdropping on this out of line, toxic man. I even pair it with a knock on the open door.

"Got a minute?" I say to Coach, not paying any attention to Oscar. Coach nods and Oscar finally gets the hint, turning and leaving, sighing like a toddler on the edge of a meltdown.

At first, I can see the guilt in Dylan's face, but he shakes it off.

"I was looking for Tyson Bishop during film but couldn't find him. Do you know if he's getting treatment or where I can find him?"

Dylan scrunches his brows, like he's trying to remember something, and then says, "Bishop requested permission to miss today. I'm pretty sure he flew home this morning."

What? He left? Without saying anything?

"Ah, okay. Cool. Appreciate it," I say and try to keep my face normal and not in the 'what the fuck' expression I feel like giving.

"Blair, have a good week off. You deserve it." Dylan smiles at me and it soothes my confusion for just a second.

"Thanks, Coach."

And then I'm out the door, trying to figure out what the hell is going on.

Me

You're already home?

everything okay?

Tyson doesn't immediately respond, and it looks like his phone is off—the messages go undelivered. My stomach rolls. Why would he do that? Just head home without saying anything? Especially because we originally were on the same flight to go together?

I'm too anxious of a person to just wait until tomorrow to fly out. Or maybe I shouldn't go at all? Before I'm in a full blown spiral, I scroll my contacts until I reach Teague's number. Not quite sure what I'll say to Ty's older brother, I can't just sit here and act like everything is fine.

It rings three times before Teague answers, and says in a hushed breath, "I thought I'd hear from you."

Nineteen

Tyson

"ARE YOU GOING TO tell me what's wrong? Or why you came back early? Or why you've been moping around my kitchen all morning?" My mom presses me, while putting her hand on my upper back, rubbing back and forth—the way she's done since I was a kid.

My mind is a blender, going from one thing to the next, but all surrounding one person: Blair. Part of me wondered if getting permission to skip practice and change my flight to get here a day early was a tad dramatic. Possibly? *Probably.* The thought crossed my mind when I was talking to the coaching staff but I needed to get out of there.

I needed to get home. To the place that's predictable and comfortable. Blair won't miss Thanksgiving and I just needed some time with my family. Needed to get my head on straight.

It's a snowy Monday in Brindlewick, Michigan. Fat snowflakes fall, making tall piles outside the windows. This is my favorite kind of weather, as long as I don't have to play football in it. Mom mulls cider on the stove and it's the smell I most associate with home. Michigan weather is a bit unpredictable, but you can typically count on it being ridiculously cold for seven to nine months out of the year. That means Mom is always making something warm to drink.

She stirs the pot of cider, her other hand still rubbing my back, and I lean on the counter next to her. This is our place. We've had many heart-to-hearts in the same exact spot. As much as I don't want to get into it, I feel my wall chipping, brick by brick, and I know I'm about to spill my guts.

And that's what I do. Over a mug of steaming cider, I tell her everything. The night at my place when Blair talked about kissing me. How weird things got after. Our almost kiss on the balcony at the Halloween party. Her crying after the game. The kiss in the elevator. And the gut punch of how she kept something like her dad calling from me but told someone random on our team.

My mom has always been the best listener. She lets me vent, almost losing my breath in the process, and doesn't ask a single question until I've got it all out on the table. Her blue eyes feel like they're looking through me, picking up all the details I forgot to say. She's always had a knack for seeing us like this.

She takes a sip of her own cider, laughing to herself, and says, "You think you're so slick. So good at keeping secrets. I've known you've loved her since that very first Thanksgiving where you used my credit card to buy a flight for a friend."

"Well, not sure it matters now," I groan, letting the steam of cinnamon and apple hit my nose.

"Tyson, I also know that she loves you. Why you can't tell this about each other is baffling to me." She exhales and then rubs her temples before locking her eyes on mine. "What did we tell you whenever you were complaining about how hard football was. How the extra training was torture?"

I take a deep breath, thinking of all the times my parents encouraged me, even when I wanted to quit. "If it's worth having, you better be ready to fight for it."

"That's right." She grabs my forearm and shakes it with her hand. "I thought you were smart enough to know that it applies to everything. Not just football."

I tilt my head, looking down at the granite counter, my fingers tracing the lines of charcoal gray on the cream stone—the way I've done ever since I was a kid.

She grabs additional mulling spices, ready for her second batch, and pours them in the pan. She stirs them with a wooden spoon and asks, "Do you think Blair is worth it?"

I pivot and catch her eyes with mine, quickly, and she already knows my answer.

"Then why are you running from the fight?"

I take a deep breath, stretching my lungs into my rib cage, before sighing out through my mouth—my shoulders following suit. "Why now? Why would she want this now? And does she really think of me like that? I don't seem like—" My brain tries to find the right word but lands on the closest. "Enough."

"Enough? Tyson. When you're ready, you're going to make someone extremely happy—you know you have this way of making everyone feel special. That's hard to find. Don't doubt yourself like that."

I nod, and look down at my fingers, following the patterns of the granite.

"And why wouldn't she tell me about her dad?"

"Sweetie, those aren't questions I can answer. But you know who can? The woman you've loved for a decade, whether you want to admit it or not. Talk to her. Be honest. At least for the sake of your friendship."

Did I fuck up by leaving her in the city? Not saying anything and hopping on the first flight? Who knows. Maybe she won't even show up? The idea of her skipping the holiday because I left her behind brings a cold sweat to my forehead.

Fuck. I'm a mess.

"I'm going to take a walk," I say while grabbing my scarf that hangs on the back of the chair. I know it's just the two of us—my dad is working and my brothers aren't supposed to be here until tonight and tomorrow morning.

"Took you long enough. We walked out there a few weeks ago. Everything is still perfect. Waiting for you." She winks at me. "Also, don't be afraid to stop by that cafe in town, Daylight Coffee, for a latte on your way back. The vanilla latte has no business being that good. And tell Skyler I said hello."

I'm putting on my coat and all the things that will keep me warm on a walk which is just under a mile when the sense of home starts to envelop me. My time in the NFL has had me living in two massive cities and while I enjoy the idea of great food and getting anything you want when you want it, I miss small town living.

Not that I want a farm or anything like that, I just want a space that's my own. No more doormen and penthouses and black cars taking me somewhere. The amazing thing about Brindlewick is there are a few coffee shops, not four on a block. You get to know the owners, they know you, and you get to chit chat about what they're working on. It's about community—building relationships—and that's something I'm going to need when I'm not playing football anymore.

The snow is deeper than this morning when I arrived and I love the feeling of the chilled air filling my lungs, biting my skin. Each minute that passes I feel more and more myself, the version I like the best. I know how important it is for me to come back here, whenever I can. I grew up in the lower peninsula, maybe forty-five minutes from Traverse City and only a ten minute drive from my parents' house to the lake.

The sound of crunching snow is music to my ears as I soak it in. The brightness of the landscape, the untouched and fresh snow ahead of me, and the pit in my stomach that doesn't feel like it could swallow me whole.

Honestly, why does it feel like I was this close with Blair, only to have it fall further away? Why does it hurt more having kissed her? Why did I leave her like that? Is all this even worth it? The questions don't stop as I continue to walk.

Then I see it. My own secret I've been keeping.

Our family cabin is first—the one where we spent endless summer days and fall nights. But then everything behind it? All ten acres of land?

That's all mine.

Twenty
Blair

I STAND IN FRONT of the door and I hate that I feel like a visitor. I've always shown up with Tyson and he obviously would just walk us into his childhood home. That isn't the case today—it's just me and a strong recommendation from Ty's older brother that I obviously still make the trip. He convinced me yesterday and I even called this morning to double check that this was still a good idea.

According to Teague, Tyson was being dramatic and doesn't know how to communicate when he needs a teeny tiny break.

Well, fuck. Tyson and I seem to be more like each other than I thought.

When the question hit me that maybe I should stay home, not join the Bishops for their Thanksgiving tradition—it was awful. It was this overwhelming wave of sadness of not playing games late at night the Wednesday before the big day, or not curling up with a warm cup of coffee in the morning, or missing out on making pie with Tyson's mom, Sara.

He's always been a consistent part of my life, even when we were a whole world apart. I refuse to accept that when the universe puts us almost in the same city, that this is where it doesn't work.

Well, maybe it doesn't work the way I thought it would. This is what I've been mulling over the whole flight. I used to daydream and wonder what it'd be like to date Tyson. Be that person. But when I thought about it, it was almost in the same way as "what if I won the lottery" or "if I could get up and move to any country, where would it be?" It never felt like an actual possibility.

Until now.

Things have shifted. We've both settled into life, as much as someone can, and it feels like the tides have turned.

And the thing I couldn't stop thinking about? Our first kiss can't be our last.

So, I created a plan—wrote it out on pen and paper—because if I didn't, I was going to be panic snacking the whole way to Michigan. I gave myself something to do and thought if I wrote it out, it'd feel more doable.

Pulling out my phone, I click my messages and find Tyson's name—he never responded, and according to Teague, his phone is off. So, here I am. Ready to put it all on the line. Or, that's what I convinced myself on the plane.

Anxiety settles in my gut as I ring the doorbell and it's only a second before it swings open, the smell of cinnamon and something sweet hitting me, and Tyson's mom beaming at me.

"Sweet girl, you made it!" she says, smiling in a way that warms me, no matter how cold it is outside. It's been snowing for a day or two, based on the snow piles from the plowed driveway. Sara kisses my cheek and wraps me in a tight hug, smelling like cinnamon. She always had a way of making me feel like I was one of the family.

"It's so good to see you," I greet her as she continues to hug me.

"Get in here. It's freezing!" She gestures for me to follow her inside. "I hope you know that your jersey is at the top of my Christmas list." Turning over her shoulder, she offers me a wink and I know she's serious.

"I want one too," Teague chimes in, wrapping me up in a hug as soon as I drop my bags in the living room. He shakes me back and forth, and says, "Or tickets, whichever."

"I'll see what I can do." I look around, trying to see if Tyson is here. I'm guessing not, considering he would've said something by now.

"He's at the cabin. Walked over there an hour or so ago," Teague says, like he's reading my mind.

Nodding, I ask, "Does he know I'm still coming?"

Teague shrugs. "I think if you didn't come, he'd be in a full on spiral. He's struggling a bit."

"Let me get you a coffee. We got some fancy beans from that coffee shop in town. And then Teague will drive you out there."

"Are you sure he wants to see me?" My voice is quiet and I dip my chin into my chest.

"Yes," they both answer in unison.

I rub my hand over my face, letting the stress of having to execute the plan I put on paper, for real.

I have a feeling that they know more than they are letting on but I absolutely don't want to talk about it with them. I'm thankful they're actually leaving it at "yes" and nothing more.

Sitting at one of the barstools, I watch as Sara makes my coffee. She puts the coffee beans in front of me to smell and my mouth is watering. It's clear where Tyson gets his thoughtfulness from. This is the kind of family where you mention you like something once and they find a way to have it for you whenever they can.

"Here you go." Sara hands me a tumbler of hot coffee, "Teague will take you."

The windows showcase the snow falling steadily, and it's gorgeous. "Actually, I'll take a walk."

IT'S ONLY THE SOUND of my steps on the snow as I make my way to the cabin. It feels like a winter wonderland, an almost completely different world even from their home. I sip coffee, notes of nuts and vanilla hitting my tongue, and soak in the peaceful surroundings—a perfect comparison to the rock that's in my stomach.

It's clear that Tyson plowed the trail they take from the house, another nod to his thoughtfulness. When I see the cabin in the distance, smoke billowing from the chimney, I stop. Truly, it's like a post card or the way you'd dream of a place like this to be. It's an honest to God log cabin, built by hand when Tyson's dad was a kid. When I'm close enough, I can see Tyson sitting inside, the curtains drawn on the expansive front windows.

My feet try to be quiet in the snow boots, not wanting to let him know I'm here yet. Needing a moment, I take a deep breath when I'm in front of the door. My fisted hand hovers before softly knocking. My lungs are tight, anxiety paired with the icy air, and my heart sprints from one beat to the next.

Here we go.

I softly knock on the door. A few seconds stretch between the knock, my gloved hand paused, like it's frozen. Excitement and nervousness pull on me, an internal tug of war.

The door swings open and there's Tyson. He's wearing a long-sleeved Henley, forest green, underneath a flannel button-up. His other hand pulls at his chin, his fingers touching the short beard. The fire crackles from inside, the only sound between us.

"You're here." His voice is layered with confusion and it almost sounds like a question.

"Of course I am."

We stand in the doorway, the cozy air warmed by the fireplace wrestling with the chilled outside. "I don't know what's going on, but you weren't at practice, and I called Teague and he—"

"You called my brother?" The blue of his eyes is intense enough it feels like gravity, pulling me closer... yet there's a flicker of uncertainty underneath, a tiny tremor that says he's not nearly as sure of himself as he pretends.

My shoulders drop from my ears and I tilt my head, taking him in, "Yes. I didn't tell him much of anything except that you left for home early. First, I had to make sure you were okay." At this realization, I lightly press a hand to his chest. My fingers can feel his sculpted chest, the rise and fall of his breathing.

He grabs my wrist and keeps it there.

"I was worried something happened. To you or back at home. I sent you messages, called, but you didn't respond. I had to call your brother."

"I didn't even think about that." His face falls, but he still holds my hand to his chest, the other hand still on the door. "Fuck. Sorry." He looks at the small amount of ground between the two of us, almost like it's an actual threshold to cross. "You were worried about me?"

Anger rains and puts out some of the nervous energy filling my body. He doesn't think I'd notice if he wasn't there? If he left me behind? "Of course I was. How can you even ask that?"

"I'm just—"

"No, don't *just* me. You know me better than that, or at least I thought you did. You know me, the real me, down to my marrow. How can you stand there and say that to me? Wonder if that's true?" My voice is louder than I hoped but anger is winning, as it should be.

How did we get here?

His shoulders hunch, the broad lines I know so well folding inward, making him look smaller somehow. His mouth opens like he's about to say something, then closes just as fast, jaw shifting like he's wrestling every word. He's a mess of 'almosts' and 'I'm sorrys' he can't seem to get out.

"My heads a fucking mess. I'm a mess. I shouldn't have left like that, without saying anything, but I needed to be home. I needed something the way I remembered it, consistent."

Consistent. The way he remembered it. It feels like my heart drops into my winter boots because I hear it. It clicks. He regrets kissing me.

I take a step back and move the hand that was on his warm chest to my hip, shifting my weight. "You know what? You were the one who kissed me. If you didn't want to, or want to take it back, just say it. Tell me. So we can salvage what's left!"

He meets me outside, our chests almost flush, "You think I want to take it back? That's the last thing I want." He raises his voice and it pebbles my skin with want.

Deep down, I know there's still more to figure out. But, in the moment, I push it all aside, letting a slow smirk pull my lips up, and challenge him instead.

"Then prove it." The words are smooth like velvet but with razor sharp consequences.

His mouth is on mine before I can even second-guess the words. I smile into it, relieved, because if he did want to take it back I think it would've broken me. Instead his lips are full, demanding, and pressing into me. His tongue sweeps along my lower lip before lightly nipping it, which pulls a whimper from me. Tyson matches it with a moan that seems to come from the deepest part of him, and I can't get close enough to him.

And like he can read my mind, he bends his knees, arms around my back, and lifts me. I wrap my legs around his waist, my winter coat awkwardly bunching up around my waist.

He turns and pushes us inside, closing the door, and sets me down. Quickly, he locks the front door and why is that so ridiculously hot? Grabbing my coffee tumbler, he sets it on a table by the doorway and turns back to me.

"Happy to prove it to you." His hand grabs at my coat zipper, slowly pulling it down while wearing a mischievous grin that could bring me to my knees. Fuck. I almost do it. But then he takes my coat off, tossing it on the sofa.

The fire crackles and pops when he kneels down, unlacing my boots. He's so close to me, to the place I dreamt of him kissing. When he looks up at me, wearing the same grin, I roll my eyes and let my head fall back, a breath escaping my mouth.

He takes his time, and it's a different type of torture. He finishes one boot and his hands move up my legs, starting at my calves and stopping at my ass, before raking back down to work on the other boot.

My hand pushes into his hair and I'm making a mental note to keep this image, him on knees like this, looking at me like that. Fuck, it's so hot. I'm turned on by a single kiss and this man taking off my boots. Can't say that's ever happened before.

When the boots are off, Ty looks up at me, "How do you want me to prove it to you?"

I can barely get the words out without begging him. "However you want."

"We might be here a while," he says, voice breathy and heavy as he slowly stands, his hands crawling up my body.

Fuck.

Twenty-One

Tyson

I HOPE I'M NOT dreaming, but if I am, I pray that I don't wake up until I get to live out this fantasy. Blair telling me to prove it? Fuck. This is unreal.

I slept here last night, after having dinner with my parents and hanging out for as long as I could manage. When someone knocked on the door, I thought it'd be one of them—not Blair. The woman of my dreams. Giving me the chance of a lifetime.

Might be messy, this thing between us, but if she's giving me any rope, I'm pulling it. Pulling her to me. Making it known what I want.

Her.

All of her.

No matter what.

Blair stands in front of me, her chest moving with quick breaths, and she bites her lip. It makes my dick twitch and I know I'm about to be hard. Every inch of her, I want to kiss. Touch. Lick. Suck. I've thought about what would happen if we ever jumped in, the places I'd start. The things I'd do.

No time like the present.

I pick her up again, letting her wrap her legs around my waist, my dick pressing into her.

"I can feel you," she teases, putting a kiss on my neck.

I slowly set her down on the edge of the sofa, my back to the fireplace.

"Do you like that you can feel me? That I'm hard just from kissing you? Thinking about what I'm going to do to you?"

Blair nods her head and pushes her bottom lip between her teeth. When she sits up and reaches forward, her hand touches the erection struggling against my jeans.

"Not yet. I've got something I need to do first." I push her back so she's leaning against the back of the couch. Hooking my fingers at the top of her leggings, she looks at me, nodding. Giving me the green light. "If there's anything you don't like, or don't want to do, just say it, ok? Otherwise I'm going to prove this to you in any way I can. Got it?"

She nods but it's not enough.

"Need you to say it, Blair."

Quick, her words tumble from her lips. "Got it."

Slowly, I use my fingers to pull down her leggings. When the front of her black panties are only a breath away, I push the pants to her mid-thigh. I put a few quick kisses on the bare skin above where her leggings rest. My lips start at the outside of her thigh, kissing until I'm on the inside. I lick up, before placing kisses the opposite way. Blair squirms as I get closer to her panties.

I switch legs, making sure there's ample room between my mouth and her center. I want to tease her. When I start kissing the inside of this thigh, she whimpers and moves into me. Lightly, I bite the inside of her thigh. Blair groans, letting out a frustrated breath.

"Talk to me." It's more forward than I intended it to come out. But, fuck it, I'm going with it. If she's going to let me do whatever I want, I'm going for it.

She swallows, the column of her neck moving with it. "Ty, that..." She stops, taking a breath in as I lick up almost to her bikini line.

"That what? Tell me." I press her.

She tips her head up and locks her eyes on mine, which are like golden flames. "Feels so good. Your lips on me."

"Good girl." I place a few erratic kisses before pulling her leggings all the way down, balling them up and throwing them out of the way. "How wet do you think you are?" I question, my lips only an inch away from her onyx panties.

"Dripping," she moans, while my hands find her bare ass.

"Is this a thong? Are you soaking through it?" I ask as I kiss the side of her ass, the skin that's there for me.

"Yes. Ty. Soaking for you."

Fuck. The groan she gets from me is one that vibrates through my whole body. I sit up and put a strong kiss on her mouth. Immediately she gives me access and I kiss her with all I have.

I pull away, my arms holding me up, one on each side of her body. She rubs my beard with her fingers and I can't get enough of her touching me.

Keeping my eyes on her, I move down her body, biting the top of her thong, and pull at it. Using my fingers on her hips, I pull her panties off with my teeth—my chin, touching her sensitive skin, and her pushing into it.

When her panties are with her leggings, out of sight and out of mind, Blair sits, legs together.

"No, no. Open up for me. Show me that pretty pussy. Let me see if my dreams have done it justice."

Blair gasps at the request but she doesn't hesitate. Her hands move from in front of her to each of her knees—she presses one open and then the other—and she's on display. I lick my lips and take her in. She's fucking gorgeous.

"Baby, you're beautiful. Now, take a single finger and tell me how wet you are."

Blair beams at being told what to do, doing exactly what I ask. Her finger moves to her entrance and dips inside, just a little. She nods and whimpers, "I'm soaked." Blair grins and arches her back at her own touch.

Fuck, that's hot. I need her to cool it before I come in my pants, which is definitely not the plan.

"No more touching, baby. Only me, got it?"

She nods and puts her arms to her side as I move in closer. I lightly blow on her clit, and watch her react with a little moan. I always wondered what she'd sound like in bed, touching her like this, but reality is so much better than what I dreamed up.

My hands grip her thighs, muscular and thick in the best way.

"I've always loved how strong you are," I praise, my hands still on her thighs.

When she squirms underneath my touch, I know she's waiting for me—fuck, I'm waiting. I put us both out of our misery and place a soft kiss on her clit. She moans, and pushes her hips into me. And I fucking live for it. For her to want me like this? The reaction? Seems like we're definitely on the same page.

I take a finger and test her wetness for myself; she's almost dripping. When I fill her with a finger, she puts her hand in my hair and lightly pulls, moaning the nickname she has for me: "Ty." Adding another finger, I pump inside her and match it with slow circles with my tongue on her clit.

Blair shakes underneath me and she uses her hands to put my head where she wants it. Almost like she knew I was going to ask her for instruction. She's showing me instead and hell, it's way better.

When I switch it up, I lick long, languid strokes from her entrance to her center, and she shivers when I get from one end to the other. My fingernails grip her thighs, scratching up and down. Up and down. But my tongue doesn't quit. I taste her, all of her, and can't wait until she's coming undone on my mouth.

"More. I need more," she pleads, all needy and breathless.

I insert two fingers and hook them, changing the spot I'm hitting, and it's the right one. Blair's abs start to clench; I can feel it in the way she's almost teetering over the edge. I nibble at her clit before devouring her. Putting all I have into her, circling, stroking, pushing my tongue into the sensitive bundle of nerves.

"I'm so close," she says as I sneak a look at her, almost losing my shit right then and there. Her cheeks are flushed with arousal, she's biting her lip, and her eyes are pressed close as her head lolls to the side.

I pick up the pace, matching her quick and shallow breaths, and when she pulls harder on my hair I know she's there—right about to tumble over the edge. Her orgasm is in sight and I moan into her. The vibrations do exactly what I'd hope for.

"Fuck, just like that. Yes!" She spurs me on.

I do exactly what she says and I'm licking, pumping, and feeling her ride out her climax. She contracts on my fingers and pulls my mouth even tighter to her. I don't stop until she's laying back on the couch, chest rapidly rising and falling with her breath.

"Ty, oh my god. That was—"

"We're not done yet," I interrupt, pressing a kiss to her mouth, her wetness still there. She doesn't hold back and kisses me, hard and promising. Her hand drifts to the front of my jeans and she rubs over my shaft, pressing into the denim.

I throw my head back, letting a breath escape me, and she kisses the column of my neck before locking her eyes on mine.

"Oh yeah? What's next?"

Twenty-Two

Blair

Oh. My. Fucking. God.

I saw our conversation going a lot of ways, but I didn't expect this. This man in front of me? This version of Tyson? The version I didn't see coming? Yes.

When I ask him what's next, it's almost like his eyes are burning into me. Branding me. Claiming me as his. And you know what? I want him to.

He doesn't answer me, so I unbutton his jeans. He watches with that same grin and devilish look in his eyes, and it's almost like it's charging me. Giving me energy—courage—whatever it is that's pushing me in this direction. I pull the zipper and then he helps take his jeans off, kicking them away.

Tyson stands in front of me, I'm still sitting on the couch, and that makes me practically eye level with his dick straining against his light gray boxers. I can even see the dot of wetness smeared on the fabric. My mouth waters, thinking about making him feel that way without him even being touched.

He made me see stars and that made him this hot? Ugh, I'm obsessed. It makes me feel powerful—even though he wanted to boss me around—and I'm here for it.

I put my fingers in the band of his briefs and look up, his eyes laser focused on me—my mouth.

"Is this okay?" I ask, making sure we're still on the same page.

"Fuck yes. You're killing me, Blair. I need you to touch me." He puts his hand through his hair, raking through the dark brown locks, and landing at his hips next where he lets them rest.

I let out a small laugh, "Someone had no problem making me wait."

His fingertips scratch my scalp as he puts his hand through my hair, before they land under my chin. "Do you want to taste me, Blair?" His voice is rough, like driving over a gravel road and it makes me throb—the hunger that was sated only a minute ago needs more.

"Yes," I answer.

He pulls his briefs down, his cock springing forward, and I need a moment. Just a second or two. Yes, Tyson is over six feet tall but I never thought about how that translated to this part of him. I'm not even sure I'll be able to take all of him. It's veiny and thick and the wave of excitement that washes over me feels like a breath of fresh air.

Can't wait to try.

I reach forward, brushing the remnants of the precum on the head, before letting my fingers graze down to his base. I can feel his eyes on me, like he's clocking every movement.

Wrapping my hand around his dick at the base, I pull a little forward and meet him with a soft kiss. It's heavy—substantial—in my hand. I can feel the groan that slips out of his mouth and I'm amazed I can make him feel like this with this type of touch—a close mouthed kiss.

Looking up, I part my lips and put him in my mouth, slow and steady. I take as much as I can, barely meeting my hand at his base, before I pull him out. I go a little further with the next pass, this time gagging.

"Fuck, do that again," Tyson groans, his hands on his hips while he lets me take control of setting the pace.

I do what he asks and try to get a little more but still gag. He's pushing me to my limit but I still feel in control—comfortable—and eager.

Setting a rhythm, stroking him and then sucking on his length in tandem, I reach my other hand up his chest. The muscles underneath are flexed, strong, and I let my hand scratch down his front. Tyson grabs my wrist and plants a soft kiss on the inside, while moaning as I work him in my mouth.

When his hands find the back of my head, he's gentle as he shifts the position enough to get a little more of what he's looking for. I know he's holding back and today's not the day to tell him to fuck my mouth the way I want him to. A girl has to build herself up to that.

"Oh fuck, you look so good like this. My dick in that mouth. Your pretty lips around it." He praises me while fisting my hair and then pulling my head away from him.

His hands are on my sides, lifting me up, and kissing me. Frantic. Desperate. Like he needs me to breathe. I wrap my legs around him as he grabs a handful of my ass with each hand.

"I'm not about to fuck you on this couch. I'm taking you to my room. Is that okay?"

I put his earlobe in my mouth, nipping it, and then say in his ear, "Please."

He kisses the crook of my neck as he walks us to his room, lightly tossing me on the bed, which must be a king considering I can spread out my entire body. Tyson reaches for the bottom of his shirt, and lifts the Henley up and over. Again, I need a moment. I've never been with a man like this, with a body built like this. He's an offensive tackle so he has to put on quite a bit of weight and good god does it suit him. His arms, his shoulders, chest—I have to make sure I'm not actually drooling.

Tyson rolls his neck and growls, "Need you to take your shirt off, baby."

No questions asked. I sit up, grab my top, and lift it up and over. The only thing that's left is a black bralette, and when Tyson nods at me, I know he wants that off, too.

Once I'm completely bare for him, he licks his lips, before hovering over me on the bed. "You're fucking unreal," he says before pressing his lips to my neck.

He moves quickly, leaving a trail of kisses down to my collarbone, and then he takes one of my breasts in his hands, the other holding him up. Tipping his head down, he puts my nipple in his mouth, and even though this is one of my most insecure body parts, Tyson doesn't bat an eye. I've never been busty, or had the sexy cleavage some women complain about. Typically, it's hard to feel sexy, but the way that Tyson looks at me, devours me, I feel like a queen.

Then he's rolling the pink bud, peaked with arousal, with one hand while his mouth sucks the other. I've never been a big fan of nipple play—more like a thing for my partner instead of bringing me any pleasure, but whatever he's doing is definitely working. Ty has me throbbing underneath him. He cages my body while worshiping me, moaning into my skin, flicking my skin with his tongue—my cheeks redden thinking about his face between my legs only a few minutes ago.

My orgasm builds and I can't believe how close I feel. I swear, the right words from this man's mouth could push me over, for the second time today.

"What are you smiling about?" he asks, pulling away from my nipples.

"The fact that you're going to make me come again," I answer, maybe too honestly.

His tongue licks between my breasts, slow and up toward me, and when he reaches my collarbone, he kisses me. Like he's putting an exclamation at the end of a sentence, it's firm and full. "Better get used to it, baby."

Fuck. I need him inside me. And when I'd typically let my partner dictate what happens next, I like to hear that groan from him when I say something he doesn't expect. And I feel like that's one of them.

"Ty. I need you to fuck me."

I was right because he lets out that groan, the one that inches me closer.

"I have an IUD. Good to go if you are." I regularly get tested when I have a new sexual partner. And I haven't been with anyone since my ex, which was months ago. Too long.

"I've been tested but haven't been with anyone in over a year," he says in my hair.

"A year?" The words come out of my mouth before I can hold them back.

He pushes himself up so we can see each other.

"The person I wanted wasn't available."

I put a hand to his chest, needing to slow this down a minute. "Are you serious?"

"Yes. So let me have you now." He dips down, kissing the sensitive skin in the crook of my neck, his hand reaching down to touch my clit before finding my entrance again. "Fuck, this needy cunt is ready for me. Isn't it?"

"If it will fit..." The concern lingers in the back of my mind, how much of him there is to take in my mouth makes it way front and center. Before I can be embarrassed, Ty's lips are on mine, searing.

"Baby, it'll fit. I promise," he insists, kissing my neck between syllables.

I reach down, grabbing his cock and say, "Then don't make me wait." I'm surprised at the needy voice that almost squeaks out.

Before I can get all the words out, the head of his dick is nudging at my entrance, before pulling out and swiping my clit. I let out another needy whimper, because this man is still edging me. My hands wrap around him, scratching down his back.

And he gets the message.

Tyson slowly pushes inside me, his dick stretching me. He doesn't go slow to tease me but for the sake that, even though I'm dripping for him, I'm not used to his size. He's holding himself up and the veins in his forearms tick with each thrust in and out. Tyson watches as he pulls his cock all the way out, and then he moves it inside me again—a little faster and further than before.

He does that a few more times and I'm grasping for him because he fills me in a way I've never felt. Each time he pumps into me, my body takes a little more, and my orgasm is within my reach. I grab my tits, rolling my nipples with my fingers, and Ty can't stop watching me. I look down and see he's almost fully inside, the painful stretch, the kind of feeling that's about to tip completely into pleasure.

"Fuck me, Ty." If I wasn't on my back, I'd get on my hands and knees and beg.

And this does the trick—flips the switch.

This time he goes faster and he's not holding back. Taking all of him feels so impossible and my body can barely register the difference between pain and bliss. Fuck, I want it all. I reach down and touch myself, for just a few seconds, getting myself perfectly primed for him to fuck me over the edge.

When I'm about to come, I reach my hands up and feel his chest.

"Come with me, Ty!" I scream as the first wave of my climax takes the air from my lungs. He watches me unravel and I know I'm squeezing around him as he speeds it up and pounds into me. I let out a guttural yell—one I'd typically cover with my hand, but I know he wants to hear it. Feel it with me.

He finds his own release and he fills me with it. Every drop of him. When he comes inside me, it's like I can grab hold of my own orgasm and ride it for even longer. Tyson shakes, yells out in pleasure, and tips his head back.

When the shocks finally subside and we're at the end, he tips his head down and kisses me, soft. This is different than before... It's compassionate, caring, and so remarkably him.

He rolls off me and pulls me to his side. I get close to him, nestling my head on his chest, throwing my arm over him.

We lay there in silence—just our breathing between us—and it's like both of us are afraid to speak. That wasn't crossing the line, that was erasing it, drawing one in a completely different place and jumping over it—together. I try to put together what happened, like if our relationship was a puzzle.

It's clear I got some of this wrong. Tyson may have always had feelings for me. Big ones. Ones where he thrives on making me come more than once. Maybe it's just that? Maybe he wants to be fuck buddies? People still do that, right?

"Blair, stop that." His voice is soft but cuts through my thoughts.

"Stop what?" I pick my head up to look at him.

He pivots toward me, a sated look on his face. "Overthinking. I can feel it from here." His fingers run up and down my arm, soothing, and he says, "Here's what's going to happen. First, we're going to take a shower. I'm going to clean you up. Then, I'm going to get us coffee and lunch. I'll also let my family know that we're alive and we'll be here for a bit until dinner. And then we'll talk about whatever is rattling around in that beautiful brain of yours."

Well, shit. He's good.

He stands from the bed and reaches out a hand. "Let's get in the shower."

Taking his hand while he beams at me like this, I can't remember a time when I was more comfortable. I notice he's staring at my thigh, so I ask, "What?"

"Just looking at me, running down your thigh, trying to keep it together." He bites his lip and pulls me to him for a searing kiss.

I try not to blush but this man and his mouth. The one I didn't know he had? It's a hell yes for me.

Twenty-Three
Tyson

THANKFULLY I HAD THE four wheeler at the cabin—the only reason I brought it was so I could plow the path from the fresh snow; I just needed something to do. After checking in with my family, I let them know Blair and I were going to hang out but we'd be back by dinner. They didn't ask any questions, which is probably best for all of us.

I'm riding back to the cabin after going to the café to pick up coffee and lunch, everything safely tucked in a thermal bag. The snow continues to fall but it's light and fluffy at this point. The wind whips my cheeks and I can't help but smile to myself, like a complete cheeseball.

What just happened? What did we just do? What does this mean? The energy sparks under my skin—trying to remember every single detail of my girl the way I had her. There's a conversation to be had and I'd be nervous if I wasn't all sex drunk from being with Blair. It was like she had me under some sort of spell. We were both so in sync with one another, not an awkward moment to be found.

And the moment I left her? I was counting down the minutes until I'd be back. She was cuddled up on the couch when I left, a fuzzy blanket around her shoulders as I threw more logs on the fire. Her eyes were hazy and skin was pink from the hot shower, like she was spent. Happy but spent.

I'm in front of the door, bag in hand, and I take a deep, slow breath. Be honest. Tell her the truth. Get it all out in the open. I coach myself up before I walk in. Letting my hand softly hit the door, mostly not to scare her if she didn't hear me, I swing the door open, thankful for the roaring fire, and see that Blair hasn't moved.

She sleepily smiles at me as if she just woke up from a nap. Kicking off my snowy boots and taking off my winter layers, I basically skip across the room to give her a kiss. Her hands lightly touch the side of my face when she kisses me back.

I pass out coffees first, both vanilla lattes because my mom was right—I don't know what they do to make these to die for but there's some sort of secret in the recipe. Then it's homemade bagels with cream cheese and a few small salads—obviously there are some treats but those are for later.

Quietly, we eat lunch, stealing glances and smiles throughout. This part feels a little bit like when you're out with your high school girlfriend for the first time, but I'm chalking that up to this shift—not just a pivot, but a massive change to our relationship. When there are no bagels to nibble on, or caprese salad to eat, we sit back, holding the coffee cups between our hands, looking at each other.

"Do you want to start? Maybe with why you left without saying any-thing?"

I figured this would happen. I know I have some explaining to do. My stomach pulls thinking about the idea of her worrying about me, how I put her through that, but also the gut wrenching news of her sharing something so personal with Zack and not me.

Her face is soft, lips full and swollen from earlier, and nervousness pulls at me. This is what I convinced myself of—get it all out on the table—I owe it to the both of us. To see if we can really make this work.

"The other night, you were supposed to come over. I had all this takeout waiting for us and you blew me off. It was like, this thing I wanted, that I almost had, was slipping away." She sits patiently, letting me get the words out. "And then it was Zack telling me about your dad calling." This is where I lose a bit of my nerve and look down at my hands, clutching the to-go coffee cup. "He knew and I didn't. Paired with our kiss in the elevator, it got me. It's all those things,"

Blair takes a deep breath, rolling her shoulders, and her eyes latch to mine. I swear I can see the reflection of the flames from the fire.

"Ty, I'm..." She looks for the words. "I'm sorry. Me not showing up had everything to do with me, and nothing to do with us." Blair points between us as we sit on the couch. "And the only reason Zack knew was because I burst into tears in front of him, it was a wrong place, wrong time situation."

"I thought we told each other everything. You can tell me anything."

"Well, it's clear we haven't told each other... everything." She tips her head to the bedroom, where we were earlier, jumping into the deep end. A small giggle skates off her lips and I appreciate the joke. "I know I can tell you anything. Honestly, I had no idea what I needed or what to do or who to tell. When you saw me in the hallway, that was the first either of my brothers heard about it and I asked them not to call my mom. It's this thing that's weird and massive, and I hate that it showed up—it's like a cut I keep dipping in lemon juice whenever I think about it."

Blair's eyes are glassy and her lower lip wobbles. Fuck. Before I can talk myself out of it, I put the coffee down and move in front of her, hand in her hair, pulling her lips to mine. She kisses me back and I pull away, sitting next to her.

"I only told Zack because he saw me on the verge of a breakdown after a game. Like, I had no choice. Holding it in wasn't an option." Her voice cracks and she coughs to try and cover it. "Then the game was awful. I was keeping this thing to myself and I couldn't do it anymore. I called my brothers when I couldn't take it. And then you saw me. And then you kissed me. And then you were gone."

My heart bottoms out at her words, the look on her face. We were both hurt, but in different ways.

"I could've come over that night. Could've told you what happened. Been honest. I just, it was all more than I could even put together. Almost like I was watching it happen to me, over and over. Not that I was actually living it." Her shoulders droop and she's drawn into herself, talking down to her folded legs, unable to look at me.

Fuck. In this moment, I know I was a dick. The realization was murky at first, maybe because I wanted to give myself more credit? Taking something that happened to her, making it about me? That's what happened. And she didn't deserve that.

"And then what the hell is happening between us? I just never thought you saw me that way. Me on the team? That makes more sense. I've always been one of the guys." She shrugs, wiping a tear with the back of her hand.

Did I hear that right?

"Blair. One of the guys? You're joking, right?!" I can't hide the eyeroll because this doesn't compute in my brain. Blair thinking I wasn't interested in her? How?

"We never had any close calls. Or I never felt like you wanted anything other than being my friend. Until recently? And there's just a lot at risk." She looks up at me, eyes full of hope.

It takes everything I have to keep my mouth shut until she's done talking. "There weren't any close calls because I knew I'd take whatever you'd give me. However, when you let me in? I was all over it. I didn't want to make you uncomfortable or anything, and fuck, I couldn't not at least be your friend."

Blair smiles, word by word, and reaches for my hand. I squeeze it and she squeezes right back.

"I've sat back and watched you date and not date, break hearts and pick yours up from the blackest of holes, and I'd do that forever if that's all you have for me. Maybe I didn't know what I felt for you, or maybe I was too afraid to come to terms with it, but it's undeniable. You're the kind of woman I thought could be it for me, and fuck, I don't know, maybe the timing is right." My free hand reaches for her chin and tips it up until I'm a breath away.

"Tyson, you don't have to—" she says, but I interrupt her. I have to.

"I love you, maybe I always have, but right now? I'm fucking in love with you. I've tried to hide it, tried saying there was someone else better for you. That you deserved more. But now, it's different. You and me, in the same place. On the same team? What if we deserve each other?"

I put it all out on the line. Ask the questions. Open my heart up and let her see all the inside crooks and crannies. And I hold my breath as the woman I love drops her jaw.

Twenty-Four
Blair

I'M IN LOVE WITH you.

Tyson just said that. Did I hear that right?

If I wasn't sitting down, I'd probably be falling over at this point. The flush of confusion and excitement rushes over my face and I can no longer hide it. Wouldn't matter because I'm sitting here with my jaw practically on the floor at this point.

Tyson loves me.

To ensure my mind isn't playing tricks on me, in some sort of orgasm coma, I ask, "You love me?"

"One thousand percent." He nods as if I asked if he needed water on a sweltering summer day. Not a single second of hesitation, his eyes bright and clear—just like his answer.

Warmth spreads through my chest, soothing the stress, the questions needing answers. The sound of the flames on the logs is the only thing between us.

"And I don't want anyone else. I tried. But even just as friends, no one else measured up."

His confession tickles something in my brain. Tyson never really dated. Sometimes we'd go out together, where our casual partners may or may not have met up with us. But there's never been someone else with him at Thanksgiving. Or other major life events. It's always been me and him. Part of me did wonder about the day he would call, tell me he met someone and he'd like to bring her home for the holidays. It felt like that day was always coming, looming in the background, but maybe it didn't have to.

"What are you thinking?" Tyson asks, picking up my hand and placing a soft kiss on the inside of my wrist. His words are soft, like I could fall into him.

"You never brought anyone else home. I sort of waited for the day you'd call, tell me about the woman of your dreams, and what that would mean." Pausing, I look at our hands, as Tyson rubs circles on the inside of my palm with his thumb. "I don't want to share you, Tyson. The thought makes my skin hurt."

"The woman of my dreams? It's you." He grins and the joy reaches his eyes, skin crinkling around them.

The weight of this circles me, pressing in from all directions. "I can't lose you. There's a handful of people in my life who are steady, a key part, and you're one of them."

"I promise, you could never lose me." He reaches for my other hand and pulls me closer to him. "I know this is complicated and it's not only my decision to make. And we have time. It's not like we have to rush it."

He means it. Only Tyson would confess his love for me and expect nothing in return. Selfless to a fault, in a way that's always made me love him the way I do. Honestly, I don't feel the pressure to make a choice. Because there's only one answer. We've been dancing around this for a decade and I don't want to waste any more time. No more dancing. No more almosts. No more wondering.

I stand in front of Tyson, only to straddle him, one knee on each side of his thighs. The grin he wears grows as each second continues. My fingertips push into his hair and I kiss him. His hands find my sides, gripping my rib cage before going around my back, pulling us closer together.

"I think we've held out for long enough," I smile into him. "I want to be with you. Only you."

He hugs me tight, kissing the crook of my neck. Being around Tyson always felt good. Safe. I knew he always had my back. But this is different. It's like finding the missing piece of the puzzle sitting on your table for far too long.

"I know this is complicated. The team. The press. I don't even know if there's a no fraternization policy? We have some time to think about what happens when we go back to New York, but what do we do when we're here? With your family?" I ask as Tyson continues to hold onto me like I'm about to slip away.

He pulls back and my fingers run alongside his jawline.

"Well, they know a little bit about this whole thing. Teague put the pressure on me the last time he was in town—trying to get me to make a move. I told my mom when I got home yesterday. We could show up, hold hands, and kiss on the couch and my family would simply scream internally, or maybe even externally. They'd keep it to themselves."

Thinking about Tyson moving around the kitchen with his mom, explaining the messy strings between him and me, makes *me* want to scream externally. A man who confides in his mom? Yeah, I'm into that.

"But, if we want to go back and act like we decided to stay friends, and that's it, I'm cool with that."

"I don't want that." I don't mean to rush the words but it's a gut reaction. The thought of playing friends, like we're playing dress up, isn't what I want. Knowing this is a safe space, with some people I love more than anything, I want to be ourselves. "I want us to be honest with them. No more close calls and almosts," he kisses my nose as an interruption, "just enjoying this time together."

"That sounds fucking perfect."

Tyson smirks into my mouth and lets out a small laugh between my lips. Pure joy. That's what I feel. In this cabin, which I've been to for the last ten years, with the man who knows me better than some of my own family members, it feels like things are falling into place.

We kiss on the couch as the snow continues to fall outside. I don't know how long we're wrapped around each other, but my stomach growls.

"Now, tell me you brought some treats back from the bakery," I whine playfully.

Tyson stands, picking me up with him—fuck, that's hot—and says, "Of course I did. You thought I'd come back without something sweet for you? I know better than that." He tips his head to the bag on the kitchen counter. "I know you, Blair Miller."

And he kisses me.

Twenty-Five
Tyson

FAMILY GROUP CHAT

Teague

earth to the love birds

when are you coming back

mom is insufferable

Mom

am not

Dad

hey hey

and she isn't insufferable

she's invested

Mom

luv you

Teague

don't forget this is the family group chat

Dad

i wouldn't

Teague

says the man who accidentally sent us a selfie when he was trying to upload a profile picture to Facebook

Dad

u never let anything go

Mom

what time should we do dinner

Teague:

whenever those two come up for air

Mom

quit it

I need to start pies. Need Blair!

or else Teague is going to have to help

Teague

SOS please come home Tyson

Dad

he's shit at pies

SOS

I can't help but laugh while picking up the phone and reading through the messages. It's only been fifteen minutes since the last one came through, so I respond, hoping Teague isn't on pie duty.

I can picture my family, huddled around each other, bickering about what I'm going to say next. That's how we've always been. Since we're all close, I feel like we know more about each other than maybe other families. I like the feeling of us all being friends, where we can give each other shit and make fun of each other. Deep down, we'd do anything for each other and that's what makes it all the more of a blast.

I knew they'd ask about me and Blair. And she gave me the greenlight to be honest with them, so that's what I do.

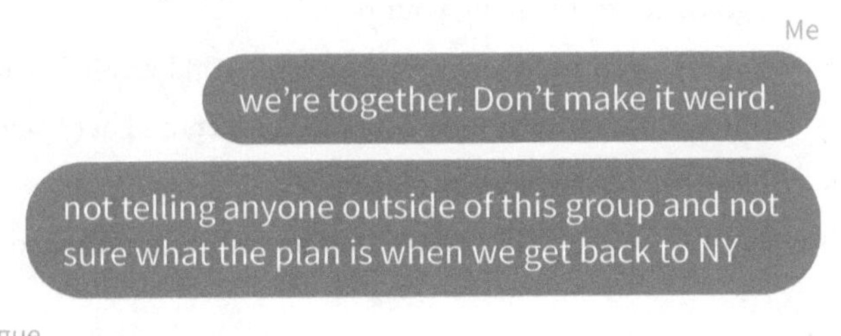

writes down temper tantrum as way to get what I want for future use

not a tantrum. And if it was, everything I learned, I learned from you

big bro

Dad

i'll be the one throwing a tantrum if we have Teague touch these pies

this is my favorite holiday don't let him ruin it

we'll be there soon.

I'm waiting to wake up from this dream but every time I pinch the inside of my arm, it still fucking hurts. This is real. I look over at a sleeping Blair—we needed a nap after our afternoon where I continued to prove to her how bad I wanted her. In all the ways, all the positions, all the time. Until we were both spent and needed a reset before dinner. Also, the second shower of the day.

"Baby, we're being summoned for dinner and prep for tomorrow. My brother is going to start making your pies."

Her eyes snap open and she throws the blanket off her. She's wearing one of my T-shirts, which is obviously oversized on her, and her black panties. Fuck... I hate that we have somewhere to be.

"You can't look at me like that!" she screeches, running to grab her leggings.

"Like what?

"Like I'm the meal!" She jumps, pulling her leggings up, and I can't help but take in the curve of her ass. I've always loved how strong Blair was, but now that I've touched and tasted most of her, it's a new level of appreciation.

"With an ass like that, what do you expect?" I lightly tap it and she pushes me away, playfully, before looping her arms around my neck and kissing me deeply. I let her tongue sweep my lower lip, tasting me until I pull away. "We really do have to go, but don't worry, I'll be hungry when we get back tonight."

The way she laughs into me? It's everything.

MY FAMILY GETS A gold star for being on their absolute best behavior. Nothing seems all that different, except for how it feels like I have so much happiness in my chest, my heart could burst. The internal thought makes me cringe, just a little, but it doesn't fucking matter... because it's true.

"Our savior!" my dad jokes as he watches my mom and Blair wrap the pies, ready to bake tomorrow. He shakes her shoulders and my girl laughs as he does it. The most perfect sound, I swear to god.

"Honey, it looks like you've been practicing!" my mom beams, looking at the final product.

"Definitely not. Not a lot of time."

"She's off being the best part of the Cosmos, didn't you hear?" Teague pokes, his wife clapping, cheering him on. "When she's not doing that, she's running her own business."

Seeing Teague hype her up like this? I love it. Honestly.

"How's the gym going, dear?" my mom asks, handing Blair a glass of rosé, who's trying to hide the pink in her cheeks.

"So good. Better than I ever thought. We can't even take new memberships right now." I zone out a little while she goes into the success of Embers and Ashes. It's not that I'm disinterested or don't want to hear, but my body needs a moment to catch up.

The stakes are high, this thing with Blair and me.

All I know is I'm one lucky bastard. I might have my hands on the type of forever someone could only hope for. It's in this kitchen, on this night, with the people I love most that it hits me.

I'm going to do everything I can to show Blair how much she means to me.

Because when you get everything you want, and more, you hold on. Tight. You don't let go.

Twenty-Six

Blair

My eyes flutter open to bright light coming in through the window, sun bouncing off the piles of snow outside. The only thing I hear is Ty's breathing and that is significant. This is the first time I've woken up on my own, with no alarm set, in I don't know how long. I'm typically running around on five hours of sleep, trying to get the things done I didn't get to the day before, or the day before that.

It feels good to slow down. Feels even better with my back pressed up to Tyson's front, his bare chest covering my back, his arm thrown over top of me. Last night, we stayed up late playing games and drinking wine with everyone at the house. It's one of my favorite nights of the year and it didn't disappoint. This morning, we'll get up, get ready and head to the house for our week-early Thanksgiving.

I stretch my legs, rolling my ankles, the weight of the snowy walk to the cabin hitting my muscles. Well, that plus *Tyson*. I smirk and blush, only to myself, thinking about the things he said, the way he *had* me, the way he *touched* me. He grabbed hold of all the insecurities of not feeling feminine enough and balled them up, throwing them further than I can see. That's one of the things I'm most surprised by.

Slowly, I move to my back, turning and watching him. His thick lashes almost dust his cheeks—it's a crime for a man to have lashes that beautiful, to be honest—and his shoulders rise and fall with his breaths. His dark chocolate locks are messy from a night of sleep and I resist putting my hands in it—I love playing with his hair.

This is really happening. And it feels big. Monumental. Potentially life changing. I'm convinced we both care too much to lose our friendship and that's what I'm holding on to. What I'm hoping for.

I need to tell him about my dad calling. Give him all the details. I need someone to be on my side. When I called my brothers, they had their own reactions and feelings to deal with. It was my experience but carried serious implications for the rest of my family. They asked me to go through the conversation, start to finish, at least three times. Asked me to check the phone log for how long we talked for. Asked for his number, as they made their own decisions on what to do next.

They asked for a lot and I get it—it's not something you expect or plan for. They were trying to absorb but also recalling their own lifelong pit of despair and disappointment. We argued about whether or not to tell our mom, and that's when I ended the call.

I was hoping for support. For listening. For them to tell me how awful it was that this happened to me, in this way, but they couldn't do it. Not that I blame them for it, but I'm not equipped to handle this on my own. But the thought of getting into it with anyone else felt like it could almost crush me.

Something else became abundantly clear: I'm still horrible at asking for help. I was practically in crisis mode, but still had everything taken care of at the gym, showed up for practice like I was supposed to, and put on the happiest face I could. Well, unless you count my almost breakdown with Zack. There are days when it feels like I have to look at my schedule and cut it up into all these pieces in order to get everything done, do everything I committed to completing.

I was getting by with slivers, not even pieces, and the weight of everything was invisible but there every time I tried to take a breath. Tried to sort myself out. Tried to mentally reset. It was pushing me further down the hill, the one I was trying to climb. And I can feel it, on the edge of myself, waiting for its next opportunity.

If there's someone who can help lift me through this, it's Tyson. Also, why is it that I'm in bed with one of the most gorgeous men, thinking about our incredible day together, and my mind immediately wanders to something awful?

Like he knows I was thinking about him, Tyson's eyes slowly open. When his lips stretch into a full-blown grin when he sees me, I'm an absolute goner. How does he do that? Make me feel this great with only a look, a simple reaction.

"Morning," he says while pulling me closer.

I smile back. "Morning."

"How long have you been up?"

"Just a few minutes." I scratch my nails up and down the arm that rests on top of me.

Tyson's eyes look like they're cataloging my features. He smirks and asks, "Want me to make some coffee?"

"No, not yet."

"Woah, you're turning down coffee. Is everything okay?"

I take in a long breath, my chest rising pushing against the weight of Tyson's arm. "I want to tell you about my dad."

Tyson slowly sits up, rearranging the pillows against the headboard, propping him up. I do the same as he says, "Okay." He reaches for my hand, squeezing it tight.

And I tell him everything. Every detail from the call. All the things I thought of. The way I was in my car and aimlessly drove. How I slept two hours before the game. Telling my brothers. He doesn't interrupt once, even when I know he wants to. His lips press together when I get to the hardest parts to say, try to explain, communicate. Tyson holds my hands when I cry, the silent tears unstoppable like a reflex.

I don't know how long we sit there for, me cracking my chest open for someone else to see, trying to get them to understand something that is so far from their experience, but he doesn't rush me. He doesn't tell me I already said something if I'm being repetitive, he truly lets me take all the time I need.

Feeling like I've said it all, I let out a breath, shaking my head, like I could lose the tears this way, and say, "That's it. That's what happened."

He shakes his head, looking at me, before using a thumb to brush the tears off my cheek. "I don't understand how someone could do that. A parent. A father. But you know what? He doesn't deserve you. He doesn't deserve to know you, call you his daughter, cheer you on from afar. He really doesn't."

I let my chin fall to my chest, listening to Tyson's words and trying to keep them straight. His fingers lightly push my chin back up, turning my face towards him, and his eyes lock to mine.

"He. Doesn't. Deserve. You. And you owe him nothing, not even a conversation. I'm sorry he put you in that position... to take something that wasn't fucking his."

These words feel like they're being spoken into my bones, like they're part of me. That's how convincing Tyson is.

I nod and wipe the tears that continue to fall with the back of my hand.

"I think the worst part was how I used to think about what it'd be like to reconnect with him. The man that was supposed to love me first. Love me forever. I always thought it'd be noble, and apologetic, and like... enough for me to forgive him for missing out on everything. But it was as selfish as the day he left. If he couldn't stay or come back, why would anyone else?"

The ultimate fear. The trauma that's followed me around no matter how many therapists I've been to. People leaving me behind.

Like the best friends in elementary that made it to high school but tossed me aside when soccer scouts started poking around at my games. Or the friends I had in college, but when they found out I was bisexual, they told me I was being greedy and had pick-me energy. The small business friends I made from the city council, but they didn't need me after I gave them all of my tips.

It's like people view me as a resource–something they can use to get what they want. Introductions to the college scouts that came to my games. The magazine who wrote an article about me my senior year in high school–sharing that contact info with other athletes. My marketing strategy for the gym because there's no way it's being successful in this economy, or so the people from my small-business cohort thought.

It just feels like there's so much about me that has turned people off. My soccer skills. My college choice. My sexuality. The small amount of success I've seen with the gym.

I know that's why I run myself into the ground, aiming to be as self-sufficient as I can be—I'm afraid to lean on anyone for things that are too important. What if they leave? Get up and decide I'm not worth it anymore. Take what they wanted and go?

Tyson's hands find my cheeks and he turns my head to his. "Blair. I want you to listen to me, really take this in." He's only a few inches away, his blue eyes like the relief of cool water on a hot day. "I am not going anywhere. I am not leaving you. No matter what, I'm going to be right here."

It looks like he's going to say something else, but he stops himself and kisses me. It's soft, full of love, and compassion, like he's telling me he's sorry. Reiterating how he's going to be here for me.

He pulls me over, my back to his front, sitting between his legs. He wraps his arms around me and my arms pull on them. Tyson's head rests next to mine, on my shoulder, as he holds me, lightly swaying us back and forth.

"I'm not going anywhere. I've got you."

And right now, in this moment, I believe him.

COSMOS SOAR OVER LONE STARS, BLAIR MILLER CONTINUES TO MAKE HISTORY

UPSTATE, N.Y.–The Upstate Cosmos came out of their bye week with a bang, storming to a dominant 38-24 victory over the Dallas Lone Stars on one of the most important Thursdays of the season. The Thanksgiving Day win, which pushed their streak to five straight, was highlighted by an extraordinary performance from none other than Blair Miller, who etched her name in league history...again.

Miller, who has become one of the most talked-about players this season, showed her resilience by bouncing back from a shaky performance the game before. Not only did she nail all five of her extra point attempts, but she also made a 25-yard field goal–becoming the first woman in league history to score a field goal in an NFL game.

The atmosphere in the stadium was electric when Miller's field goal sailed through the uprights, and even the away crowd couldn't help but cheer on the historic moment. Fans from both sides stood in admiration of Miller's achievement, acknowledging the significance of what she had just done.

The Game Day Tribune

The Cosmos' victory, which saw them secure two late touchdowns in the final two minutes, was a testament to their resilience. Despite the Lone Stars' late surge, the Cosmos' defense–alongside Miller's steady leg–helped keep the game in hand as the clock wound down.

With the Cosmos now 5-0 since Miller joined the team, it's clear that the rookie's presence has made a lasting impact. According to the Cosmos' front office, they're working on finding free agent and practice squad kickers to join the team as they make a run at another Super Bowl. The league is watching closely as Miller's historic start to her career... wondering what comes next?

Twenty-Seven
Tyson

TODAY WAS MY FIRST Thanksgiving game and I could get used to this. At my old team, we were never picked for the coveted prime-time slot, which meant we usually got to go home for actual Thanksgiving, but I'd trade celebrating a week early if that meant I get to play in something so monumental to the game of football.

It was one hell of a game and a day that will be tough to forget. We were just on some good shit, on all sides of the ball. The type of day where everyone was locked in, and it was a complete shootout—lots of points from both teams, going back and forth. Games like this are one of the things I'll miss most when I decide to hang up my cleats—the energy, the sideline, the camaraderie.

Watching Blair kick a field goal and fucking make it? Un-fucking-real. I've been in a lot of stadiums but hearing the sound when it went through was unbelievable. Fans from both sides were in awe, excited to be part of history. The camera crew was ready because they got all the shots of the little girls wearing Blair's jersey.

Do you know how hard it was for me not to pick her up and kiss her on the sideline? Keeping our relationship a secret was something we decided was non-negotiable. We didn't need to make this more complicated, especially when Blair has all this attention with the Cosmos. We can keep it under wraps.

If you told me I'd end up dating a best friend, I'd have never believed you. But here I am, racing home from the win, so Blair can meet me at my place. We've had one night together back in the city, but I never realized how busy Blair is with the gym. I'll take what I can get as we try to figure out what this looks like back in New York.

Tonight's going to be a good one, considering tomorrow is a no-alarm-morning for Blair. She has things to do at the gym but it's not time sensitive. We've tried to find a few days like this coming up, so we can spend more time together.

The doorman buzzes in, letting me know a visitor is here, and I know it's Blair. She softly knocks at the door, even though I told her she could come in when she got here.

I swing the door open to see a fresh-faced Blair in leggings and an Embers and Ashes crewneck. She has a bag with her and I have to hold back my excitement—I told her to bring some stuff so she's comfortable when she stays over.

She kisses me on her way in, locking the door behind her. I grab her hand and spin her, which has her laughing, before saying, "You were incredible today."

"Stop it. You've seen me kick a whole bunch." She tries to wave off the compliment.

Pulling her to me, my hands on her low back to press her hips into me, I continue, "Do you know that for all time, you're going to be the first woman who played on an NFL roster? Scored in a game? Made a fucking field goal? No one can take that from you." I put a kiss on her forehead and she grins. "Baby, I'm so glad you're here."

"You just saw me," she laughs into our kiss.

I dip her playfully. "Not like this I haven't."

"What are you thinking for tonight?" She sets her bag down and looks me up and down. The thing about leggings is that they're dangerous when it comes to women like Blair. She's all muscles, curves, and things I want to grab hold of.

When she rolls her shoulders, a little grimace on her lips, I ask, "Are you sore?" An idea starts to form.

"Yes, my shoulder blades, and I don't know what Dylan had me doing this week, but my legs are actually tight." She grabs her foot, pulling it to her ass in a hamstring stretch, standing on the other leg.

"How about a massage?" I suggest.

She practically melts. "Yes. Let's do it."

"Then we'll order dinner," I add, not letting her know it might be a late one.

"Perfect," she says as I reach for her hand, walking her down the hallway and into my bedroom.

Kissing her, I push her lightly down on the bed, before getting the massage oil from my bathroom.

"Wait, you want to use oil? Won't it ruin your sheets?" She runs a hand over the fabric.

I reach down and take my shirt off and Blair's eyes immediately go to my chest. Fuck, I love it. "I'll get new sheets," I shrug. "You can't have a massage without oil." She nods. "Now, lose some layers and lay on your stomach."

Blair pulls off the crewneck, a light purple lacy bra covering her. Next is her pants where she reveals a matching thong, the same color lace. My mouth is practically watering watching her, standing at the edge of my bed.

She smirks at me before laying down in her bra and panties, turning her head to one side. I stand on the edge of the bed, getting on my knees on the floor—a perfect place to start. I pour a little oil into my hands, rubbing them together to warm it before placing them on her calves, starting with her legs.

As soon as I press my fingers into her skin, one quick pass, Blair shivers, a soft groan escaping as I start kneading her muscles. The tension pushes against me and she lets out that little noise whenever I get to a sore spot.

"God, your hands," she breathes, voice muffled slightly by the pillow.

"You love these hands, don't you?" I ask as I reach further, my arms extended and touching the start of her hamstrings, right above the soft skin behind her knee.

"Yessss—" she draws out as I push into her muscles with my thumbs on each of her legs.

I spend a few minutes on her calves and feet, the oil slick and warm against our touch. When I get to the sides, she moans in a way I'm familiar with. She's so sore that she doesn't know if she loves it or hates it.

"Were you on a stability ball this week?"

Blair pushes herself up on her forearms, looking back at me over her shoulder. "That's why! I couldn't put my finger on—oh my goddddd." She puts her head back down as I run my knuckles up the side of her calves, trying to release the tight muscle.

After a bit, she settles in, not nearly as sensitive when I touch and I can feel her relax. I move to the bed, in between her feet as she's sprawled out on my bed.

I warm more oil between my fingers and work the backs of her thighs.

"I'm serious. You're so good at this," she says in a euphoric way.

"I'm good at a few things," I suggest, moving my hands from her legs up to her ass. The thong has her creamy skin on display. Starting on the sides, I incorporate it into the pass I'm doing with her hamstrings—right above her knees all the way to the sides of her ass.

"Why don't you show me?" Blair tempts and it's all I need to explore. To see how far we can go. Together.

And then I move away from her legs. I grip her, my fingers holding the sides of her ass, and let my thumbs massage the skin right outside the fabric of her thong. Up and down, harder and lighter. When I pull my hands from her, she moans, not in pleasure but the lack of pressure. I'm not touching her.

"Come back," she whines.

I take my mouth and kiss the place where her cheeks start, still rubbing her with my fingers. When my mouth touches her, she clenches, for just a second. Switching sides, I mimic my movements and I feel her squirm. Smirking into her, I give a light bite.

"Fuck, Ty."

"Do you like when I touch here?" I rub my thumbs inward on the top of each thigh, which has them ending up close to her entrance.

Blair whimpers. There's my answer. I do it again, testing the limits and going a touch further. I move my hands down the back of her legs, scratching, before I place soft kisses up her ass, near the fabric.

As I kiss and nibble, she lifts her hips a little off the bed. Noted.

I reach forward, grabbing her hips and lift her up and towards me. "Get on all fours for me, baby."

She does what she's told, and the new angle has me kissing, licking, touching closer. Her body moves and pushes against me—she likes it.

"Such a good girl. Do you want me to take these off?" I hook a finger at the top of her thong, pulling it up and away from her body—changing the pressure of the fabric on her clit.

Moaning, she says, "Yes."

I pull them down until they're stretched between her knees. When her ass is bare, I sit up and push my erection into her... near her hole. Blair whines when I touch her, even though there is fabric between us. I grab her ass with both hands and ask, "Has anyone ever had you here?" I press my thumb onto her sensitive hole, just enough pressure so she knows what I mean, and she shivers.

"No," she says out of breath. But needy. Wanting.

"Would you like that? Me kissing you. Licking you. Fucking you in this tight little hole?" I press a little further, to see her reaction.

Her head turns, and then she's looking at me, "Yes. Fuck, yes," she practically cries out.

I remove my finger and give a soft kiss to a cheek, "Not today, baby. But soon, I'm going to claim that spot, only for me. You got it?"

"Yes. Ty."

Without warning, I plunge my tongue in her entrance, tasting her wetness. I swirl my tongue and then lick all the way, close to her hole, but retreating before crossing that line. When I do it again, Blair whimpers when I retreat. My beard grazes the inside of one of her thighs and she says, "I love your beard. The way it prickles my skin."

A devilish grin spreads on my lips, one only I can feel.

"If you love it so much, why don't you sit on it?"

Twenty-Eight
Blair

"WHAT DID YOU JUST say?"

"You heard me. Take those panties off and get over here," Tyson commands as he lays on the bed, head on the pillows like he's waiting for me. His hands go behind his head and a tiny blip of nervousness hits me.

I do what he says and then crawl on the bed, kneeling between his legs.

"Don't make me beg," he teases.

"I might be too heavy. I don't want to like... suffocate you," I say, letting my insecurity out in the open.

Tyson sits up, brows knitted together. "Baby, I'm a professional athlete. I can lift your entire body weight. Believe me, you're not too heavy. And suffocating while eating you out? Talk about a good way to go." He smirks, laying back, and his confidence is contagious.

There's a pool of need thrashing low in my belly, desperate for him.

Before I can let my brain bully me into anything else, I slowly crawl up, grabbing the headboard with my fingers. I go to lower myself on his face but his hands grab my thighs and pull me to him.

"Oh!" A startled sound creeps out of my mouth. I've never done this before and even though he's reassuring me that this is what he wants, doubt still lingers.

Then he touches me with his tongue. He's at my entrance, moaning when he tastes me, and he licks all the way up to my clit. Slow. Steady. Patient.

A moan falls from my lips, my hands gripping the headboard.

His tongue is flat on me when I gently move my hips. I move enough to feel his beard on me, the friction that inches me closer to my orgasm. It's unlike anything I've felt before. The softness of his tongue, paired with the roughness of the skin around his mouth is fucking unreal.

I feel the doubt fall from me, the want for more taking its place. Ty's fingers dig into my thighs as he works me. His tongue laps at me, long and slow, and I swear I feel him moan into me.

My knuckles are white, my hands gripping the headboard, holding myself up a little and reaching for my climax. I take a chance and look down. Seeing Tyson like this has the knots in my belly tightening, the strings pulling against each other—watching him is ridiculously hot.

His eyes find mine and I'm caught. Watching. Riding his face. And enjoying the hell out of it. He doesn't stop, even as I take in every one of his movements. His hands rub my thighs until he spanks me with one hand, the other digging into my ass on the other side. The soft fullness of his tongue is a perfect contrast to the sharp stinging.

Inching me closer, my heart thumps in my chest, echoing throughout my body. I rock myself forward, looking for the friction of his mouth, the roughness of his facial hair.

"Yeah, baby. Ride me," Ty moans before immediately going back to work.

His voice is like velvet, soft and something you can fall into, but devilish enough that it feels like a dare.

My body responds, picking up the pace, and then it's me hitting just the right spot. It's like there's nothing else in this world but me, Tyson, and the headboard. Waves wash over me, my orgasm pricking at all the right nerve ends. He doesn't quit; he keeps licking and nipping at me, pulling me closer to him, being part of every single shock.

"Tyson!" The scream that leaves me is surprising. I've never been that vocal in the bedroom, but with him everything is different.

He keeps tasting me, all throughout my entire orgasm. When I've crashed out, top to bottom, and am nothing but a panting, satiated mess, lying next to him, he straddles me.

Tyson's eyes pin me in place as he says, "I love when you scream my name." He smirks and then leans down, my wetness on his lips, and kisses me. It's one of the most intimate moments, like it's truly just the two of us. Any of the self-doubt or questions has fallen away, and I don't think they'll be returning.

Tyson is one thing I'm 100% sure of.

Twenty-Nine
Blair

WHEN CLAIRE, MY MANAGER, asked if I'd be interested in an interview for an upcoming article written by one of my favorite sports writers, the answer was *hell yes*. It would only take a couple of hours, and even though it impeded on my training time, the Cosmos front office was excited. The reporter and their crew came to the practice facility to interview teammates and some of the coaching staff, followed by a quick lunch off-site.

Being included in one of the most prolific sports magazines to ever exist wasn't something I thought I'd ever get a chance to do. I'm so excited to see how it turns out and am already thinking about what I'll do to commemorate. While I'm thinking about how I'd deconstruct the article from somewhere in the middle of the issue to frame it, my stomach flips. It comes out today and I can't wait to leave practice to get a copy.

We're in a team meeting about to be dismissed for the day when Coach Dylan takes the podium. Before he can say anything, Zack yells, "Everyone be quiet, it's a big DILL..." The team laughs at Zack's pun, including the coaching staff.

He holds up a magazine and everyone starts to cheer. My face is on it. The cover. I'm not just *in* the magazine, they gave me the *cover*. My body is frozen; I don't know what to do. This isn't what I expected. I hope the guys aren't pissed.

Dylan tells everyone to quiet down as he reads the headline, "Blair Miller: This Is What a Game Changer Looks Like."

And then the coaching staff are passing one out to everyone. *Oh my god.*

Zack stands, his copy in hand, and says, "Blair! YOU'RE ON THE COVER!" His enthusiasm is contagious and everyone starts to clap.

The heat on my cheeks is aggressive and I know I'm about the color of a tomato at this point. I look to find Tyson and there he is, smirk tugging on one corner of his mouth, and he claps for me, before mouthing "Wow" and giving a thumbs up.

The cover slides in front of me as one of the coaches claps me on the back, offering a massive smile. There I am, on a magazine cover for something I've had a subscription to since I was a kid. My brothers and I would argue about which pages, showing our favorite athletes, each of us got to keep to put on our bedroom walls or doors.

But now, I'm on it.

What is this timeline?

Coach Dylan comes back over the mic. "Only want to keep you a few minutes longer, but this deserves our attention. Blair deserves our attention."

I feel like I could melt into my seat. I thought I'd get some random high-fives in the hallway or the gym once people read the article, not a team meeting shout out.

"The article is fantastic, but I'd like to read just a few lines." Dylan says, before opening the magazine up to the sticky-noted page. "For years, the NFL has asked how to grow its audience. Blair Miller showed them—by expanding who's allowed to dream."

Everyone is dead silent as they take in Coach's words, some even flipping to the page where the article starts. I can do nothing but stare at Coach in the front of the room. He pauses, looking up to me, wearing a look of pride it'd be impossible to forget.

"It may have been a bizarre sequence of events that brought her here, but it's her tenacity and drive that everyone should be taking note of.

Assimilating to a male dominated sport, from the players, to coaching staff, to the front office, is something that's never been done. And people are paying attention. With her jersey being the best seller of the season, even with her joining in week five, you can taste the shift in the league. The idea of looking for talent and game changers in the places we wouldn't expect. Blair Miller may be wearing an Upstate Cosmos jersey but make no mistake— she kicks for all of us."

Coach closes the magazine and sets it on the podium. The people sitting around me give high-fives, shake my shoulders, hit their hands on the table in front of me. All of them are excited.

"Blair flies under the radar. She's never late, doesn't miss anything team related, and she had a whole life before this all started, including a successful business. I just want to say how proud I am. Of her, this team, and this organization for doing something that's never been done."

I'm going to pass out. This can't be happening.

The room claps. I see the head coach, my teammates, some of the best players in the National Football League, cheering me on.

"I'd like to say something," Benny requests, still in a cast but starting to join team meetings while he's working on his recovery. Everyone turns their attention to him, the guy who is supposed to be the secret weapon on special teams, one of the most sought-after kickers in the league before his injury, as he adds, "Blair, thank you. When I went down..." He looks at his leg and continues, "I felt like I let *everyone* down. But then you appeared. And I don't know what it is about you, but it's like you've got some magic or something. We're having a hell of a season and we couldn't have done it without you."

Benny claps, still standing. And one by one, everyone stands to join him. Until I'm the only one sitting. It's overwhelming. I'm about to cry for sure. And the amount of encouragement in this room? My god, it's what I hope for every athlete.

It feels like they want me to say something, and maybe that's what will end this. As amazing as it is, being the center of attention is never my go-to.

Slowly, I stand and I swallow past the tears that are threatening to spill. I wouldn't feel bad about crying in front of my team, especially after this showing of appreciation, but I try not to.

"Thank you. This is all," I look around, taking in the whole room, impossible to catalog all the faces, "very kind. I just want to say thank you for letting me in. I know how hard it is to be part of a team but I have to say, you all made it so easy. Thank you for that. And, Go Cosmos." I shrug my shoulders as the room erupts into cheers.

Coach Dylan lets us go and I wait for the room to empty before walking down towards him.

He greets me by reaching out a hand, I take it, and he shakes. "Blair, you're one hell of an athlete. Be proud of this."

Then I hug him. It's the only way I can think to really thank him.

"Thanks, Coach."

"She didn't just become the first woman to score in the NFL—she became the reason girls now imagine themselves in cleats, not just in the crowd," Mags says while we're on a FaceTime call, her face fills my Mac-Book—I needed the bigger screen for the bigger conversation.

Covering my eyes, I say, "I know. I KNOW. The article is ridiculously good. Like, I didn't even think I was this cool." I play it off.

"Would you stop? This is amazing! You're on the cover. Have you seen all the stuff online?" Mags' excitement is something I can feel, almost like if she's in the room.

"No, I've been avoiding it. I can't take it. Good or bad."

"Well, let me give you the highlights. First, a bunch of teams in the NFL are trying to plan youth camps for girls. They're trying to introduce them to football and other sports earlier and at the same caliber as the boys. Amazing! And I'm sure you've heard about the donations to Athlala." She plays with the end of her long blond ponytail.

I shake my head, knowing nothing.

"Ever since your article was released, Athlala has received almost a million dollars in donations from professional sports teams and athletes. They love the mission. Love how you got your start with the gym. These are not small peanuts things... These are life changing, needle moving improvements."

My mouth hangs open and I shimmy my shoulders, trying not to cry. "Wow. I don't know what to say."

"You don't say anything! You take a minute to be proud of yourself."

"Okay, I'll try."

"Well, besides all of this and you and Tyson tying the knot, what else is new?" She pokes fun, sticking her tongue out at me.

I roll my eyes, close enough to the camera that she can see it. I don't even know where she's at currently—professional tennis keeps her jet-setting all over the world.

"Actually, I'm looking at a location next week. For the next Embers and Ashes. One is a spot in Manhattan and the other is in a city about forty-five minutes from here."

Mags' eyes are wide and she claps, the sound a little delayed through the screen. "Damn! Look at you... dreams coming true and all that."

"I'm just hoping I can sustain this. I won't have another check from the NFL but I do have some brand meetings next week. Claire's excited about a few of them, maybe because she'll finally cash a check."

Mags laughs. "Claire doesn't work with anyone she doesn't want to. Believe me. She can be picky. Lean into her, she's one of the best managers around. Plus, she's not hurting for money, I know that much."

"Okay, enough about me. Tell me, what's new in the tennis world."

I'm desperate for a topic shift—I'm not used to this. While Mags jumps into the latest tennis drama and happenings, there's one thing I can't stop thinking about.

I know I'm lucky. Part of me wonders when my luck will run out.

Thirty

Tyson

Mom

oh my god blair is on the cover!!!

Dad

wow

Teague

wow is right

Me

isn't she amazing? The article is so good

Mom

can't wait to get my copy

and brag to everyone that I know her

can you send us jerseys yet?

we don't have any extras yet, I'll check with the equipment manager though

Teague

My cheeks pinch from smiling. I knew they'd be excited. And then there's Teague, bringing up marriage when we've been dating for a few weeks. Sounds about right. Time might move differently when you've been friends for ten years, but it doesn't go to marriage in a month.

I walk into the bar, looking at my watch—3:00 PM right on the dot. I'm meeting a potential contractor for my land in Michigan. When we stayed at the cabin, I kept thinking about how nice it would be to have family over for holidays. Or even being that close while able to stay at our own place.

That feels like years ahead, but building a home is a process and I don't want to be waiting on that to finish if me and Blair are ready sooner than that. Or maybe it's just me. I don't know. We've not had the future talk—we're very much operating in the now—but I'd do anything to keep her in my plans.

Now, this meeting was a complete surprise and something that happened in the last twelve hours. I hadn't even had a chance to talk to Blair about it, but the contractor reached out to say he had an opening six months sooner than originally planned. I did try and text her but she had something come up with Embers and Ashes' second location and was giving me the details. She needed me to listen–this could wait.

I check in with the host stand and they take me to a table where one of the best contractors, according to a few guys on the team who have built homes, is already seated. I know they'd never lead me astray, and for what I'm looking for, I'm confident it's pretty tame compared to what some people want.

"Tyson. So good to meet you." He stands and shakes my hand. "Glad we were able to connect on such short notice."

Sitting, I reply, "Absolutely. Thanks for reaching out."

"Okay, I know we're on a bit of a time crunch, so tell me about the land and ultimately what you're trying to do."

Opening a folder, I pull out a few pieces of paper. "It's a small town—Brindlewick, Michigan. I bought ten acres right behind our family cabin. I want to put the house an acre or two back. Here's a map with the topography and lot lines." I hand him a map and continue. "Not looking for anything super extravagant but something big enough. Two stories, not including a finished basement. Thinking three thousand square feet. Five bedrooms, enough bathrooms... you get it. In the back, I want an in-ground pool and hot tub. A small personal gym, but shouldn't need a shed or anything like that."

"Any thought to the visual style?"

"I like a farmhouse structure, or something similar, but don't really want it to look like a farmhouse. Like, I don't need the black and white color scheme. I want something different."

He nods, nothing catching him off guard.

"Is there a partner who will be helping with these decisions, or is it just you?"

I smile, nodding along. "Umm, yes. Probably? We can include her from this meeting on, as long as she wants to, if that's okay?"

He nods, grinning down at the table, like he gets it. "More than okay. This is great starting information." He gestures to the folder. "When are you hoping to break ground?"

"As soon as we can. It's not urgent; I'm still in New York for a bit, but I want it to be ready for me as soon as possible. Even if it's not our full time address."

"You got it," he confirms. "I'll work on these next steps and start putting together some floor plans for you to react to."

And just like that, the land I bought years ago has a plan.

Thinking of the future, outside of football, makes me feel good. Prepared. Like, more of a person outside of the game I've been fixated on my whole life. It's always been football—the team you're on, the contract you've signed, and where you could end up. While I'm definitely lucky to have only played for two teams during my entire career, I've never been the one calling the shots—where I landed was always in the hands of someone else.

It feels good to think about taking control. How much physical turmoil I put my body through. When is the last time I'll step on a field as a player? Not sure when that will be because I honestly don't have a date in my mind, but I like the idea of thinking about it early. No matter what, that day will hurt, and having my own place and part of a plan will lessen the pain. Or, at least I hope so.

Excitement for sharing this secret with Blair cuts in and I know I'm grinning like an idiot. My phone buzzes.

Teague

how did it go

did you discuss putting in a pool that can be used all year round?

Me

No lol

it was good. Basic starting meeting

can't wait to tell Blair

don't freak her out

you guys just started not being idiots

i'm not going to freak her out

you don't even have anything to show her yet

i'd wait

like don't you have enough going on. Big matchup tomorrow

I didn't think about that. There's not really anything to tell, or show. If there's a moment where it feels there's a natural opening, I'll tell, but if not... I'll wait until I have a little more.

Teague hasn't ever given me bad advice. Well, as an adult. When we were kids, he used to tell me all types of shit that was hilariously horrific. Like when he was getting me to layer puka shell necklaces the first day of ninth grade. Or, when he said that guys who danced with girls at the dances were stupid–that one I figured out halfway through homecoming and ended up being the talk of the grade.

Maybe he's right about this, though?

Thirty-One

Blair

"This feels weird," I say, holding hands with Tyson in the car as we pull up to the practice facility.

He squeezes my fingers with his. "No one can see. We're friends, plus it's not your fault that your car needs work done."

I roll my eyes at his fabricated lie and let my head fall back on the head rest, catching his wink just in time. Grabbing my travel coffee mug, I down the rest of the brewed cup—a special blend that Tyson got me for my birthday, one I finally opened. It's a dark roast, rich and smooth, and like it has the ability to make me run faster than usual. I love it.

Coach Dylan asked for me to come early so we could have a quick meeting and it seemed to perfectly align with Ty's in time, so, carpool? Save the planet and stuff, right? Or just not be able to pull yourself from your boyfriend long enough to have time to go home and get your own vehicle.

Boyfriend. Even though the internal thought catches me off guard, the smile hits my lips as I turn and look out the window. We're walking towards the staff offices, which is on the way to the men's locker room, and it sounds like someone is getting their ass handed to them with the door open. Tyson looks at me, brows furrowed. We're only a few steps away and there's clearly something going on in there.

"We should go," I suggest, grabbing Ty's arm and trying to turn him.

He shushes me. "Wait. I heard your name." Waving me over, we get closer to the door, and try to listen.

It's not hard to hear, considering the person doesn't know how to speak at a reasonable level. And immediately, I know who it is.

Rolling my eyes, I lean in and whisper, "It's Oscar. Benny's loser agent or whatever."

Tyson's brows raise. "How do you know that?" He leans in, still trying to listen.

"This isn't the first time I've heard him complain about me. The day you left for home early, I was trying to check with the staff, seeing if you were getting treatment or something, and he was in here doing the same thing, or that's what it sounds like."

"What's his problem?"

"Now? I don't know. Previously, he was mad about me taking up his client's roster spot."

"That doesn't make any sense. Benny's out this year."

"Right, that's what Dylan told him. After he kicked him out of the office."

"What the fuck?" The look on Tyson's face is priceless.

We get close enough, keeping our steps quiet, until we're right outside the doorway.

"Just come clean. Who did you pay for this article? This feminist trash? How'd you do it?" Oscar demands, in a way that makes me want to kick him straight in the dick, if we're being honest.

Dylan scoffs. "You are a real piece of work and I mean that as disrespectfully as possible. We didn't pay anyone. The magazine reached out to Blair's manager. I told you that."

"This is such bullshit. Why are you leaning into this? She's nothing other than a washed-up collegiate athlete, a dime a dozen." Oscar yells over Dylan, then slams his hand on something, probably the desk. "Benny wants a trade. If you're going to keep entertaining this, he's going to walk. Choose between your future hall of fame kicker or your PR stunt that's dragged for long enough."

And before I can stop him, Tyson is walking into Dylan's office.

"You've got some balls coming in here, talking like that, don't you?" He gets chest to chest with Oscar. "Why don't you keep going?"

Dylan immediately gets between them. Turning to Tyson, he says, "I need you to go to practice, don't give this idiot the time of day. Believe me."

Oscar jumps in. "I heard that!"

Dylan turns to him. "Good. You were meant to."

This whole thing is ridiculous. Someone who I've met one time is threatened enough to come into my place of work and complain about me being here. He's trying to make me feel small, like I don't fit.

When Dylan uses the intercom to call security, Oscar looks at me, head to toe, and snarls, "You're not even close to being worth it."

It doesn't sting in the sense of what he's saying; right now, it's the fact that he thinks he has the right to say anything. Just because he's someone's agent? Or manager? Where do these men find the audacity?

"I'd rather talk to a wall than give you another ounce of my energy, Oswald."

"It's Oscar."

"Don't care," I laugh, thinking about how he called me the wrong name when we first met.

There are more things I want to say, actually kind of want to scream, but Dylan stands in front of me.

My coach sighs. "Tyson, Blair, go. Get to the weight room or something. I'll find you."

I pull at Tyson's arm and we leave. We're only a few steps away from the door when we pass security. People pop their heads out of their office to see what's going on as Oscar shows he has no dignity and continues to spew his bullshit when he's being walked out. My name is still fresh on his lips.

We walk down the hallway and my head tips down, watching the floor in front of me. A pit opens in the pit of my stomach and a wave of nausea washes over me. I hate that I heard him; that I had to tell Tyson this wasn't the first time I've had an interaction like this. Hate that Dylan had to call security for a grown-ass adult. And hate that it feels like I'm doing a walk of shame in the place where I was so excited to come to today.

Sure, I've had one interaction with this man, where I barely put up with his shit, but he was awful. Acting like he didn't know my name, doing things I've dealt with my whole life. People trying to make you feel like you don't fit or you're not here to take up space? Those who question your ability because of what you look like? Keeping opportunities from you because you don't fit the mold? It's fucking exhausting.

I've dealt with guys like Oscar my whole life. On the field. In the gym. At the damn grocery store. The kind of men who puff up the second they feel small next to a woman, or anyone, with a bit of talent or confidence. Apparently, the thought of me being part of this, around his client, was too much.

Tyson's quiet beside me, but his fists are balled, his jaw working. I know he's biting back words. Not because he's afraid to say them—Tyson is never afraid—but because of me. Because he's trying to respect the fact that I hate a scene.

"Blair," he starts when we're finally alone, standing in front of the weight room door, "you know none of that shit was true, right?"

Leaning against the wall, I cross my arms, trying to keep my voice steady. "Doesn't matter if it was real. It still happened. Still made everyone stop and stare."

He reaches out, grabbing my shoulder. "They weren't staring because they believed him. They were staring because you were handling it. They were watching a woman who wasn't afraid to take up space. Also, because he's the fucking worst. I've heard enough and seen enough—there's no way the front office staff will let him back in the building."

I look away, blinking fast. I know he means it. I do. But I also know what it looked like—the way I shrank, the way I couldn't even meet anyone's eyes in the hallway.

"I hate that he made me feel like I don't belong here. That he makes me question if it's a PR stunt or if it's real. Feels like I keep having to prove I belong here. Like it doesn't matter how many reps I hit, or plays I run, or hours I put in. There's always someone waiting to tell me I don't measure up."

Tyson's hand slides up to hold my cheek, gentle and full of care. "Then they better get used to the sight of you measuring past them." I lean into it, even though we shouldn't be doing this here. He pulls his hand away, realizing the risk. "Don't think about one loser in Coach's office. Think about the entire team who cheered you on after the article. The stadiums are full of fans cheering you on, even when they're wearing another team's jersey. All the little girls you're inspiring."

I feel something crack open in my chest, the realization that no matter what, people like Oscar will exist. They'll try to take others down simply because they think they can. It's barely about me and mostly about them.

Doesn't mean it still doesn't sting.

Tyson stands and offers me his hand. "C'mon. Let's lift something heavy until the world makes sense again." The man comes in when he knows I need an out from this situation. He knows me.

He holds the door open as some people wave at us from their stations or machines. I smile back and try to keep my chin up, but I'd be lying if I felt like the same athlete in the parking lot.

Right now, I feel a tad smaller—like the walls stretched up and the floor tilted just enough to remind me I'm standing on someone else's turf.

Thirty-Two

Tyson

THE STADIUM ENERGY IS still buzzing under my skin when the clock hits zero. A three-point loss and our first of the season. It shouldn't feel like a victory, but hell—if there's a way to lose, this was it. Two heavyweight teams trading touchdowns, and according to the coaching staff, we're the two favorites to go to the Super Bowl.

I adjust the tape around my ankle, feeling the tight burn under the wrap. It held up better than I expected–didn't really feel it until the second half.

We jog toward midfield, helmets off, ready to shake hands. I clap a few guys on the shoulder pads—good game, respect, all the usual. But my eyes keep drifting across the line.

The opposing sideline is a slight storm of bodies circling one person. Blair.

She's got this exhausted but proud smile, like she knows how important her role was in every point we put up. The opposing team crowds her, tapping her helmet, grabbing her shoulders, yelling whatever praise she probably won't believe later while she's overthinking the film. She lifts her chin a bit, and the stadium glow hits her face just right. Fuck, she's gorgeous.

I'm supposed to be shaking hands, but I slow down a step just to watch. It looks good on her—being celebrated. Being wanted. Being seen. Especially after our run-in with that dick bag, Oscar. I called Benny that night, told him what happened, and he made sure to have a conversation with Blair about it.

I know he's on her side. Just like most of the players. This moment is one of my favorites from each of the games since Blair has joined the roster—when they all get to meet her.

Blair catches me watching her and it's like time stops. Everything slows, the guys introducing themselves, people being in awe of what she's accomplished. It's just her.

Here, from the sidelines, I know I'm looking at my future.

THERE'S A SOFT SHUFFLE outside the door and then the faint scrape of paper against carpet. My heart leaps straight into my throat. Grabbing it, I see a room key with a note:

Shower in 5

-Blair

My stomach flips, like I'm at the top of the rollercoaster, looking over the drop. I look at the time and nervously wait for the five minutes to be up. I keep running my tongue over my bottom lip before pushing it through my teeth.

When it's been five minutes, I crack the door open an inch, peering down both sides of the hall and checking to make sure none of my teammates or coaches are around. The coast is clear, and I can feel the relief wash over me, like when you get to sit after your first long practice of the season.

I close the door fast, leaning my back against it, pulse drumming through my ribs. The hotel logo glares at me from the keycard inside as I walk towards her room. We're on the same floor but she's quite a few away.

I round the corner of the hallway and then I'm in front of her room. Quickly, I use the key to get in her room, hoping no one sees me. Swinging the door open, the adrenaline of sneaking around and being in Blair's room has me smirking. The sound of the shower running, steam creeping from the cracked door leading to the bathroom, has me ripping off my clothes.

When I step in the bathroom, lavender and peppermint kisses me with the steam.

"Hey you. Right on time." Blair's voice is velvet on my skin.

It's not long before I'm in the shower with her—the woman of my dreams. Fuck, I know I'm a complete goner and I wouldn't have it any other way.

Blair wraps her arms around me, her body pink from the hot water. We stand there for a few seconds and it's hard to believe this is actually my life.

"Sorry about the game," she almost whispers as her head rests on my chest.

"Not even on my radar," I reassure her.

It's true. A close loss like this would've been hard to swallow previous seasons, but honestly, seeing her on the field after? Being with her now? Sucks to lose but it's not the end of the world.

"You don't need a distraction?" she questions while pulling away, her lashes fluttering around her honey colored eyes. Blair leans in, her lips finding my neck, and I lean away to give her more room.

"If you're the distraction, I always need one." If I sound needy, it's because I am. There's no limit on how much of her I can take. How much I need. My time with Blair is never enough.

She stands in front of me, her body fucking perfect. The curve of her thighs. The slight dip of her waist. Her round ass. It's enough to make me hard. When I go to reach for her, give it a stroke, her hand grabs my wrist.

Slowly, she goes down on one knee, and then the other. "No, it's my turn." Her lips are a breath away from my length.

Her fingers wrap around me, stroking from base to tip, nice and slow. Her eyes catch me looking at her—I swear, she fucking soaks in the gaze like I'm praising her.

She drags her tongue across her lower lip, painfully slow. Back and forth. When Blair places the softest, barely-there kiss to the head, I can't help but give her a moan.

Pulling away, she has me leaning forward, wanting her to touch me with her mouth again. The push and pull of control—something we both love. She takes a breath, her hand still working me, before taking her tongue to the tip, giving it a swirl.

She has me in the palm of her hand. Literally.

Her lips kiss from the tip down to where her fingers grip me at the base. I think she's going to make her way back, but instead her tongue laps at my balls. She takes one in her mouth, hums, and my knees almost buckle.

"Fucccck." The word drips from my mouth like the bead of precum about to make itself known.

Blair asks, "Do you like this?" She does the same thing with the other, her tongue working me.

My voice wobbles when I try to answer. "Fuck. Of course I do."

She switches her hand and her mouth—her hands lightly cup me while she licks up the base of my shaft.

Her hands then reach around the back of my thighs, holding her steady while she's down on her knees. She opens her mouth and I take the initiative, fisting her hair while I slowly fuck her mouth.

I try not to go too fast but end up making her gag a few pumps later. "Sorry, baby," I apologize, pulling out and giving her a second to regroup.

"Don't apologize... I won't break. Fuck me." Her eyes are devilish and her voice is like a siren calling me.

"You're fucking incredible," I murmur while slowly entering her mouth.

Her lips close around me, her fingers digging into the back of my thighs. Pulling her hair a bit tighter, I thrust in and out of her mouth—she does her best to take me.

Blair moans, the vibrations surrounding me like her plump lips, and I'm teetering. Fucking close to coming in this perfect mouth.

One of her hands gives up the leverage of grabbing my thigh and cups my balls while she sucks me and that's all it takes.

My balls tighten with my climax and as I start to come, Blair moans like she loves it. She takes it, every drop, lips around me as the shocks hit me over and over.

I'm panting when she pulls away. Before she swallows, my hands still in her hair, I say, "Show me." And my good girl opens her mouth—my release sitting on her tongue.

"Now, swallow," I demand.

I watch the muscles in her neck and see as she takes my release. Then I pull her up and place a searing kiss to her lips.

"You're such a good girl, Blair," I say and she kisses me back.

Who cares if you lost a football game when this is who you're coming home to?

Thirty-Three

Blair

I COULD GET USED to this. We're laying in bed, all exhausted from the game, and trading orgasms in the shower. Tyson is playing with my hair as I lay across his chest, and this is next level happiness.

"Benny called me," I say, needing to talk about the thing with Oscar.

Tyson's fingers don't stop as he asks, "Yeah? What did he say?"

"Sorry. He apologized for Oscar, even though I told him he didn't need to," I explain.

Benny was almost chaotic on the phone. He kept tripping over his words, telling me that he doesn't share Oscar's views, and how he would never say something like that. The second I met Oscar and Benny at Zack's Halloween party, I knew Benny was a quality human while his agent was not.

"I know he felt bad. He brought it up in the group chat with some of the guys."

For some reason, that makes me feel a little better. Not because I want Benny to suffer, but because the guys know about it, and don't agree with it. I could tell word started getting around because of the way the guys were going out of their way to check in on me—even guys I don't typically work with or see at the facility. I appreciated the support.

"I did tell Benny that I'm not planning to try and play next season." This has Tyson's hand dropping, and him sitting up in the bed. I follow suit and continue. "This has been fun. Amazing. Challenging. One of the most important opportunities I've been given. But this season will be enough for me, no matter where we end up."

Tyson nods, a smile on his lips. "I'm just so fucking proud of you." He pulls me closer to him, putting a kiss on the top of my head.

"Well, I have some news." I take a big breath and get ready to tell Tyson the thing I've been dying to share. The thing that just came together. My stars are finally aligning and giving me direction for early next year.

He raises his brows, waiting for me, and I can't help the way my cheeks pinch with a smile.

"Embers and Ashes is getting a second location. I found the perfect spot in the city. And now is kind of the time to jump, with the popularity of our original. Athala approved it and we're starting the renovation next week." I know I'm talking too fast, the excitement rolling off me.

"Blair! This is amazing!" Tyson cheers, eyes wide and bright. "You are fucking incredible."

"Really owe it to the Cosmos, honestly. The max-out in memberships and waitlist for classes really helped build a business savings the last few weeks."

Tyson's brows pinch when he says, "No, you owe it to you. It only exists because of you."

"This thing with Oscar being so threatened by my presence is almost funny, considering I'm not even going to be a factor next year."

"Well, you're not going anywhere. We'll find a way to get you on the field to watch a game whenever you want," he insists, pulling me in for a kiss.

I laugh into it and feel lighter. I haven't kept this to myself long but we haven't had any conversations about what happens after the season. I'm thankful that I have a clearer path for after this. It's always been about getting the gym to the next month—make enough money for the rent and to pay the staff. And every month I was able to do that was a win.

While this opportunity with the Cosmos has been truly remarkable, it's really shown where my passion lives. I want to create a space for everyone to feel safe and supported when they work out. The idea of creating more opportunities for young women to try new sports makes me excited, like I can't wait to get to work. I can do that with multiple gyms and use this NFL stint as a stepping stone into what's next.

"And, if you need somewhere to stay in the city, I think I know a place," Tyson practically gushes.

Then I ask the question I've been wondering for a while. "Are you disappointed? That I don't want to try to do something with the team?" I brace for the answer I'm afraid of. For me to let down someone in my life who means so much.

"How could I ever be disappointed? You changed your entire life for this. I'm thankful we've had this time but it's like a gift. I figured that would be the case." He looks at me in a way which reinforces his words. I know he's being open and honest.

My muscles loosen, giving up some of the tension. I stretch my neck, side to side. "I'm excited for what's next," I say and then look to him. To the man who makes me feel like I can do almost anything.

"Me too, baby." His lips meet mine, soft and full. I love when he calls me that. I've never been one for nicknames. My ex-girlfriend tried it once and I physically recoiled when the word left her mouth. With Tyson? It's different. It's right.

"Maybe you can work for me when you're done with football?" I joke, pressing a finger into his chest. "Stay in the city near the new location. Teach spin classes on the weekend?"

Something crosses his face, his eyes darting around, before landing back on mine with a weak smile. He opens his mouth, like he's going to say something, but he doesn't.

"I'm kidding, Ty. You don't have to work at the gym." I reassure him because I can feel the tension between us. I don't know what it is but there's no part of me that wants to press it. Maybe he hasn't thought about what happens after football.

And right now? It's not the time. I don't need this piece of him as we're close to sleep and a special kind of tired.

"I think you forget how bad I am at spinning." He lolls his head to the side, laughing to himself.

I match his energy but lean my head into his shoulder. He's not wrong. I remember the first time he came to a class with me in college and it was surprising. Spin bikes have a different type of finesse and it felt like Tyson had never been on a bike of any way shape or form.

"I love you, no matter how bad you are at it." I place a kiss on his lips.

Tyson kisses me back and says, "I love you, too."

We sink into the king-sized bed, his body curled around me, his arm heavy over mine and I know I'm about to have the best night's rest in a long time.

Thirty Four

Tyson

ANOTHER WEEK GONE IN the season and I feel like I'm on cloud nine. After our loss in the previous week, our team has been on fire. Everyone pushed harder, dug deep, and cheered each other on.

We were away this week and even though our team was supposed to be the underdogs, we obliterated the other team with a final score of 42-7. Blair was perfect for extra points and with each one she made, it felt like the crowd was louder than before.

Blair's at my place more often than not. She's been taking meetings in the city for the new location and also letting Tiffany step up and get a taste of what her new leadership position could look like.

I'm amazed at how quick Blair's brain moves. She's always considering the next move. Making a decision for the question that hasn't even been asked yet. She's an unstoppable force.

I'm unlocking my door when my phone buzzes.

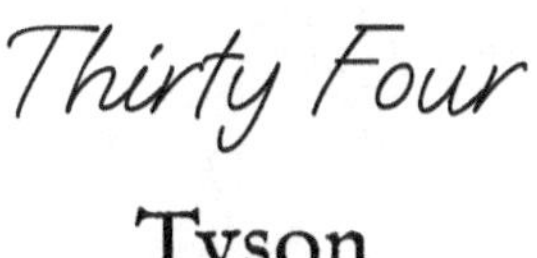

I drop my bags and open the app to get groceries. Once I pick out everything we need and schedule the delivery, an email from the contractor comes through.

Apparently, there's an issue with the flood insurance—something about being too close to the water? Seems like the plans are a no-go until we figure this out. I call my dad, and he tells me he remembers that being one of the question marks when they built the cabin back when I was a kid.

The contractor lets me know there are still a few options to explore, but everything's on hold for now. He doesn't seem pissed, but I feel kind of dumb, like I should've had all this checked before. I don't know... I've never built a house before.

I'm just glad I didn't prematurely tell Blair about the potential house. There's no need for her to worry or spend any energy on something that might not even happen. December in the NFL means we're getting closer to knowing playoff seeding and hoping for another championship. Plus, there's the very successful business she's running and planning to launch next year.

I'm really proud of everything she's taken on.

But Teague is right—there really isn't anything to tell yet when it comes to the potential house in Michigan. At least for now.

Maybe I can figure it out and then share it with her when it's more concrete. Because even if the floor plans aren't, I know one thing for sure: Blair is my future.

COSMOS KICKER PARTS WAYS WITH AGENT

UPSTATE, N.Y.– Benny White, the Cosmos' injured starting kicker, has officially parted ways with his agent, Oscar Williamston, citing differing visions for his career.

"It was a tough decision, but Oscar and I just see things differently moving forward," White said in a statement released Friday. "I'm grateful for what we accomplished together, and I'm focused now on getting healthy and coming back stronger next season."

White has not played since breaking his leg in the first game of the season, an injury that sidelined him for the year. The team expects him to return as the starter in 2026 once fully recovered.

In his absence, Blair Miller has taken over kicking duties, becoming the first woman to play in the NFL after the Cosmos' two backup options fell through. Miller's historic debut has drawn national attention and widespread praise.

Despite the setback, White remains upbeat about his future. "I love this team, and I can't wait to be back out there," he added. "Right now, it's all about rehab and getting ready to help the Cosmos win again."

Thirty-Five

Blair

A GRIN PULLS AT my lips as I arrive at Embers and Ashes—coffee in one hand, keys in the other, a whole list of things I wanted to tackle before sunrise. The gym always looks a little sleepy this early, like it's holding its breath before the day kicks off. I love it like this. Quiet. Mine.

But this morning, something feels... not quite right. At first, I can't place it as I walk to the front door. Something uneasy settle in my gut in the darkness of an early December morning.

Then I see the front window.

I stop walking. My keys dangle from my hand but my coffee hits the sidewalk, painting the snow and cement. The glass is shattered—spider-webbed, like someone had gone at it with a bat. And across the front, black spray paint screams at me in blocky, uneven letters. **FUCKING BITCH.**

Closing my eyes, I take a few breaths—hoping it's just a dream. But when I open them, the glass is still broken, and the spray paint is every-where. Looking up, I see the name of my gym is also shattered, many of the lights no longer working.

My gym. The place I built. Fought for. The thing I've poured into for years of my life. My safe space which no longer feels that way. I look around, making sure no one is watching me—a typical feeling for most women simply trying to exist.

Taking a step closer, broken glass crunches under my sneaker. When I get closer to the front door, I find it's red spray paint this time, **NOT WORTH IT**, smaller but still clear as day.

My stomach drops as the realization hits me but it's not even that surprising. *Oscar.* Or someone Oscar got to do his dirty work. There's no way this is a coincidence. Honestly, it has his cowardice all over it. His smirk, the way he couldn't handle a woman taking up space. I should've known after the way he acted at the facility—that weird possessiveness about football, about grilling Dylan about the *real* reason I was there.

This is different. It's not some dumb insult thrown across a practice facility or said loud enough that everyone could overhear. This was calculated. Violent.

I can't move. My legs felt stuck in place, like if I walked any closer I'd see something even worse. My hand grips the strap of my bag so tightly my knuckles hurt. A thunderous heartbeat, one too fast, fills my ears as I try to catch my breath.

Putting my key in the lock, I slowly open the door, afraid someone may be waiting inside. I'm only a few steps in when I realize it's untouched. Nothing looks out of place but instead like a typical morning, one I've had a hundred times.

Inside, it still looks like my gym. But right now, it doesn't feel like it. And that's what does it—this is what sends me over the edge. I dial 911 as tears stream down my face. As the operator answers, I rush to lock the door and turn on all the lights inside.

How is it in the place that I've built and designed, from scratch, no longer feels like my own?

I'M TAKING THE ELEVATOR up to Tyson's place. After calling the police and dealing with the media—who couldn't move fast enough to get pictures of the damage—I'm completely spent. As if that weren't enough, I just got off an emergency call with the Athlala board to discuss what happened and what this means for the future of our expansion sites. They decided to postpone any work or plans on the new locations, just until things calm down, maybe until we have answers.

I didn't tell them I already have an idea who did it. That's between me and the police. After explaining my run-in with Oscar, paired with Benny firing him, the officers agreed it was enough to question him—and with help from Dylan and the Cosmos' front office, maybe even get a search warrant.

It's only eight in the morning, but it feels like I've already lived an entire day. When I called Tyson, he was out for breakfast with Teague. He told me to go to his place and that he'd be back soon.

The moment I close the door behind me, a wave of relief hits. I breathe in slowly, trying to steady myself. If I think too hard about everything, I'll spiral. I just need a few quiet minutes—let the insurance company call, take the next step, one at a time.

I move to the kitchen, dropping my bag on the counter, and notice something rolled out across the bar. Blueprints. Or something close to it. I'm not snooping, not really—but when I see an envelope sticking out from underneath, curiosity wins. I pull it out.

Tyson—here's the first couple of ideas for your property in Brindlewick.

Brindlewick. His hometown. *His property.* My heart dips. What property? Since when?

I look closer. The plans show layouts, a map, and some land markers. His parents' home. The cabin. And right next to them—a new plot, labeled *Tyson Bishop Residence.*

He's building a house.

I'm still staring at the lines on the page when the front door opens. Tyson rushes in, practically out of breath. He wraps his arms around me from behind, squeezing tight.

"Baby, are you okay?" he asks.

I turn on the stool to face him, holding the plans between us. "What's this? Because It looks like it's by your parents' place. In Michigan."

His expression shifts—just a flicker—but I catch it. He takes a slow breath. "Fuck. I didn't know Teague pulled these out," he says mostly to himself. "I was going to talk to you about it—"

"Talk to me about what?" My voice isn't sharp, but it's tired. "You buying land? Building a house? You relocating? Seems like we have a lot to talk about."

"It's not what you think." He moves closer, his voice soft. "I don't even know if the land is buildable yet. The contractor sent me those before he did his checks. Nothing's set in stone." Tyson's voice wavers, and he takes another step like distance itself might ruin his chance. His hands lift, then fall uselessly, caught between reaching for me and not daring to.

"So... it's just an idea?" I ask, but my throat feels tight. "Because from here it looks like you've got blueprints."

"I took one meeting. And if you asked the contractor, he'll tell you, I mentioned doing this with someone else. You," he says quickly. "I was going to tell you, I swear. I just didn't want to bring it up until I knew if it was even possible."

I want to believe him. I really do. But I'm so tired—of press calls, of questions, of always holding things together. The thought of one more surprise, one more thing I didn't see coming, makes my chest ache.

"I just wish you'd told me," I whisper. "Even if it was nothing yet."

"I get that," he agrees, reaching for me. "I didn't mean to keep you in the dark. I was trying to figure it out first, before making it a whole thing. It's just land, Blair. No walls. No roof. Not a decision. Just... a maybe."

Something inside me breaks a little when I think about Embers and Ashes. The new location. My current gym. How the hell would I do this if I didn't live here? "Do you believe in me?" I ask quietly.

He looks confused. "What? Of course I do."

"Then how could I run my gym, the one I've spent years building, if we're suddenly in Michigan?"

He opens his mouth, but nothing comes out. And that silence... it's worse than an actual answer.

I look down, tracing the edge of the paper. The plans blur as my eyes fill. "Everything feels like it's falling apart right now," I admit quietly. "And I came here hoping this—us—would be the one thing that still made sense. Felt steady beneath my feet. But I feel like I've been blindsided."

He steps forward, voice soft but firm. "Hey. We *do* make sense."

For a moment, I want to let that be enough. But my heart is raw, and logic doesn't feel like comfort. His words sound like he's talking underwater. I'm overwhelmed and my brain can barely put this together after everything with the gym.

A strangled laugh sarcastically falls from my lips. "Really? Because none of this makes sense to me."

He doesn't move, but I feel it all the same—the ghost of being left. The absence takes a shape long before it arrives. My body remembers what my mind keeps denying. It doesn't feel like he's choosing me, and it's the thought that could bring me to my knees.

The tears stream consistently down my cheeks, like the throbbing ache that's threatening to crack open my chest.

"What do you need?" His words land soft, but they scrape raw. Like skin that never got the chance to heal right.

The air feels too thin, like I'm breathing through gauze. His words echo somewhere beneath my ribs, deceptively sharp, and I can't tell if it's grief or just fatigue making me tremble. "I just need a minute," I tell him, backing away. "To breathe."

"Blair, please—"

"Not forever," I say, shaking my head. "Just right now."

My feet move before my brain catches up. I focus on the sound of them—heel, toe, heel, toe—because thinking means feeling, and I can't afford either.

"I love you. Don't go."

The words hit the back of my neck like heat. I close my eyes for half a second, swallowing the instinct to believe him. I've believed too many people who didn't know how to keep me.

I stop, hand on the knob, but I can't turn around. "Then just... don't keep things like this from me," I say, voice barely above a whisper. "No matter what."

The door shuts between us, and the silence on the other side feels heavier than his words ever did.

The Game Day Tribune

BLAIR MILLER'S GYM VANDALIZED FOLLOWING HISTORIC NFL PERFORMANCE

ASHBURY, N.Y.– Cosmos kicker, Blair Miller, arrived at her gym, Embers and Ashes, early Tuesday morning to find the exterior vandalized.

Spray paint across the windows, smashed windows, and a damaged sign marked a targeted act that sources close to Miller describe as "personal and deliberate."

Since opening, the Athlala-owned gym has been more than a place to work out–it's been a safe, welcoming space for women to build strength and confidence through functional fitness. A trusted part of the neighborhood, the gym also plays a major role in local fundraisers and community causes.

A member who asked to be anonymous shared, "Embers and Ashes is a place where everyone is welcome. Good days. Bad days. There's always room for you here. Well, not to whoever did this… you should have the day you deserve."

The Game Day Tribune

No one was injured and the interior was untouched, but the message was clear–an attempt to intimidate a woman making waves in professional sports.

The Ashbury Police Department has launched an investigation. Surveillance footage is being reviewed, but no suspects have been identified.

We reached out to Blair Miller and The Upstate Cosmos' front office–both have declined to comment.

The studio is closed this week as the damage is assessed.

Thirty-Six

Blair

SNOW DRIFTS PAST THE window in lazy spirals, the kind that hushes the city. Inside, the radiator hums, filling the quiet I can't seem to. My reflection blurs against the glass—pale, tired, the kind of tired that lives in your bones.

"Blair?"

I blink back into focus. Dr. Latham's voice is calm, steady, like she's used to pulling people out of this heavy fog.

"Sorry," I mumble, shifting on the couch.

"That's okay," she says, crossing one leg over the other. "Why don't you tell me about your dad?"

The question catches me off guard. "My dad?"

"You mentioned he called recently."

I huff out a dry laugh. "Yeah. First time in over a decade. And not to say he misses me or anything. He wanted football tickets." I pick at the nail polish that's almost chipped all the way off. "Guess being in the NFL finally made me useful again."

My therapist waits, letting the seconds stack on top of each other before asking, "How did that feel?"

I scoff and let my eyes look around the room. The feeling is still there—the way I felt when he used the nickname from when I was a kid. It was like I was holding a hot pan, feeling the scorching on my skin, but couldn't find a way to let go.

"Horrible. And crushing. I always had this hope that one day, he'd show up and apologize for being gone, give me a good reason. He took that from me," I say, my throat tight. "I should be used to it by now. But it's like—" I stop, trying to find the right words. "Every time I start thinking maybe I'm enough, something proves I'm not."

Dr. Latham's eyes soften. "You feel like you're not worth it?"

"Maybe," I admit quietly. "Earn the offer. Earn your spot on the team. Earn a day off. Earn the right to be at the gym. Earn the right to take up space." I keep picking at my nails, afraid to look at her when I sound so pathetic.

"Blair," she says softly, "Mitchell doesn't get to decide what you're worth anymore. No one does. Your worth is up to you."

I immediately smile, hearing her shift from calling him my dad to his first name. Because, no matter what, he's really not my dad. The words land harder than I expect. Not sharp—more like weight, like truth settling where it needs to.

She leans forward. "He only has power over you as long as you keep giving it to him."

I swallow, blinking fast. "So what, I just stop caring?"

"You don't stop caring," she says. "You stop chasing. You stop proving. You learn to cope when the feelings arise. That's how you take your power back."

Something cracks open inside me—not in a dramatic way, just a quiet release. "I'm so exhausted. Like, I'm one thing away from completely melting into the floor, unable to stand back up.

Dr. Latham's pen stills. "Is Tyson the tipping point?"

Tyson. Hearing his name makes my stomach twist. It's been two days since I left his apartment. We've texted—short, careful messages—but it's not the same. Every time my phone buzzes, I want it to be him saying *come back*, but I was the one who needed space. I was the one who said I needed to breathe. Still, the quiet between us feels heavy. I miss him in a way that sits behind my ribs, dull and constant.

"I really don't think Tyson meant to hurt me," I admit finally. "In all the years we've known each other, he's always been there. Ready to help. Ready to pick me up."

Dr. Latham nods slowly. "Sometimes people protect what they're afraid to lose. Keeping it to himself may not have been about control—it may have been about fear."

Her words land gently, like snow against glass. I think about the way Tyson's voice cracked when he said he was sorry, how his hands shook when he tried to explain. He wasn't scheming. He was scared. And maybe that's what caught me so off guard—I thought I was the only one afraid of losing something real.

"I guess I wanted him to see me as a partner," I share. "Not someone who needed shielding."

"Maybe he does," she says softly. "But his version of care isn't yours. You can love someone and still misread what they need."

I exhale slowly, the ache in my chest shifting into something smaller, something almost manageable. "I hate that that makes sense."

Dr. Latham looks at her watch, "And I hate to tell you we're almost at the end of our session." She closes her notebook and leans back in her chair. "It doesn't have to make it right. The pain," she says. "Just understandable. And understanding is what lets you decide what to do next—not hurt."

I nod as her final words run over me, like the comfort of a blanket. Outside, the snow thickens, muting the world to gray and white. For a moment, I just watch it fall, the quiet pressing soft against the window.

Maybe that's what this is—not forgiving too soon or holding on too long. Just learning where to go next. And who to go there with.

When I step out into the cold, the air bites at my cheeks, but it feels clean. For the first time in a long time, the weight I'm carrying feels lighter and a little more like mine—not something I have to earn.

"YOU'VE BEEN HOLDING OUT on me," Maggie teases, her face filling my laptop screen. Her face is as soft as her voice sounds—full of love and understanding. I wouldn't expect anything less from my best friend.

My video feed shows a pretty rough version of myself: red eyes, blotchy cheeks, and an empty wine glass–only a few drops of rosé left.

With Maggie's training and tennis tournament schedule, we've not been able to get into everything. Until now. She obviously knew that Tyson and I were a thing, but being able to dish on all of it feels so cathartic. Everything from the away game to my run in with Oscar at the facility, to the gym details and the fight with Tyson.

"And then I feel bad about missing the game–"

"Blair. Stop. You're allowed to rest. To cope. To take a minute for yourself. Some loser with probably the littlest dick to ever exist vandalized the gym. I bet the team understands you need a few days."

I let out a laugh and my fingers rub at my temples. It's quiet between us—just another reason to love Maggie as much as I do. We can yap for hours on end, or we can virtually just do our best to be there for the other.

"I miss you. I wish you were here."

She grins. "I told you, use some of that fancy NFL money and book a flight. I'm going to Australia to play in a tournament in just a few days."

"When the Cosmos season is over, it's a deal."

She claps her hands and dances on the screen, shimmying her shoulders and making me laugh.

"What do I do about Tyson?" The question comes out rushed and almost a little desperate.

Maggie gets to the screen, her brows pinching together. "That man is not going to leave you, Blair. Take the space you need. He's loved you for a decade—you think this is going to scare him off? Please." She crosses her arms and leans back.

"You sound so sure," I muse, taking a quick peek at the window to find snow piling on the windowsill.

"Well, I have an advantage, you see..." She rests her head on a hand propped on the table, like she's a daydreaming teenager. "I've seen the way you both look at each other. Like there's no one else. That's how it's always been. So yeah, I'm sure."

My cheeks redden and I pour another glass of wine. I need something to do with my hands.

This thing between me and Tyson has never been about earning anything, but about finally letting something happen that was always there. Not earning it, not proving it—just *allowing* it. Like we've both been walking around pretending not to know the ending to a story we've already read.

I take a sip, the wine catching in my throat. "It's complicated," I murmur, though what I really mean is *it's terrifying*.

She smiles, that slow, sure kind of smile that makes you feel seen. "Of course it is," she says. "That's how you know it's real."

Thirty-Seven

Tyson

I LINE UP ON the practice field, but I'm not really here. Not in the way I usually am. My hands are ready, my feet remember the defensive set, but my head's somewhere else. It's back at my apartment with Blair. I can't believe I left the floor plans on the bar. I got them the night before and I was just so fucking excited—it all felt so real. My brain was trying to think of a meaningful way to get them in front of Blair. Tell her that she's part of this decision because I want her as part of my future.

Now, it's been a week and we haven't talked. I called her brother to make sure she was doing okay, and he told me she was struggling, but that it wasn't anything she couldn't handle. The thought of her going through this vandalizing thing on her own has been fucking eating at me. Chomped at open wounds and made me wish things were different. I want to be there for her.

Blair missed Sunday's game. Coach called it "strategic rest," but I know the real reason. She needs space. Space from me. Space probably from the sport that brought the damage to Embers and Ashes. Without a kicker, we tested our ability to go for two after every touchdown, and it's clear we're still not strong in that area.

Apparently, Oscar is maintaining his innocence but no one is buying it, especially not Benny. Shortly after Blair and I had our blow up fight, he came to my apartment and wanted to know everything I knew about

Oscar and Blair. Apparently, Coach Dylan gave him a heads up, and then the police paid him a visit.

The whistle cuts through the air and I'm slow to start the play. Our head coach sees it, because let's face it, nothing gets by this man, and he yells, "Bishop! Get your head out of your ass or get the hell out of here."

I nod in understanding as he tells us to take a quick break. I blow out a slow breath as I jog off the line. Zack jogs up beside me, flipping a ball in the air. "What's your deal today? I don't ever remember you being this horrible..." he presses.

I grunt. "Just tired."

"Bullshit."

Glancing at him, I want to push back, but he's not wrong. I don't have the energy to wear a mask. We walk off the field together, cleats crunching on the practice turf. I sit on the nearest bench like I'm suddenly carrying twice my weight.

There's a pit in my stomach I haven't been able to shake. It's not just the space between me and Blair—it's the secret I've been carrying around like a damn anchor.

"I should've told her," I admit quietly.

Zack sits beside me. "Told who what?"

"Blair," I say, running a hand over my face. "About the house."

He frowns. "What house? Icy Tyson, you're not making any sense."

Slowly, I take in as much air as my lungs can hold. I know I'm about to come clean on everything. I can't keep this to myself. "The one I'm going to build in Michigan. By the lake." I stare straight ahead. "I wanted to start breaking ground in the off-season, even if I didn't make it my full time address for years. I thought I was doing something smart. Something long term."

He lets out a low whistle. "Damn. First things first, that's serious. And second, *please* tell me you and Blair are a thing, because I've got a bet going with Emilie that I'd very much like to win." Zack rubs his hands together like he's just cracked the code.

I don't answer him but I give him a look, one that he reads like a book. He claps his hands, and cheers to himself.

"She came over to my place after everything happened at Embers and Ashes and saw the plans sitting out."

His face, mostly playful, drops at that last confession. "Well, shit."

I lean forward, resting my elbows on my knees and spill my guts. I tell him everything. Zack listens intently, asking questions as I go through it. When I'm done, he lets out a low whistle and it just reiterates how I screwed up.

"I was going to tell her. She just saw them before I could do that. The timing was off. She's building something amazing here in New York with her gym, her career. She's finally getting the recognition she's always deserved, and I didn't want her to think I expected her to give that up. I thought if I just waited... maybe we'd figure it out together."

Zack doesn't say anything right away, which is rare for him. After a few seconds, he says, "Or maybe you were afraid she'd say your futures don't line up."

Fuck. That hits harder than it should.

He stresses, "Do they?"

"Honestly? Now that I have her, I can't imagine anything being more important than that. I'd do anything for her." I let my head fall in my hands.

"You mean it," Zack says, almost a little surprised. He looks around, still just the two of us, and leans back. "Also, I fucking knew it."

"She thinks I don't believe in her dream," I say. "Like I've got one foot out the door. And maybe I do—just not in the way she thinks. Like, she could tell me where we are going next and I'd make it work."

"Damn, wish you would've just told her, huh?"

My look is as sharp as my words. "Obviously. If you have the ability to go back in time, let me know. I'd pay big bucks to do so," I joke.

"I am a very talented individual, I know." He dramatically puts a hand to his chest, "But, even I haven't figured that out."

I appreciate the crack in the heaviness of the conversation. We sit for a few seconds, taking in the practice space around us.

"I love her," I say, and my voice goes tight. "God, I love her. I've always loved her. Now it feels like things are finally aligned, and we have a real shot. But I don't know what to do."

Zack stands up, tossing the ball between his hands. "You do know what to do. Don't play dumb." He gives me a long side glance.

I look up at him.

Rolling his eyes, he exhales a dramatic breath next to me on the bench, his shoulder bumping into mine. "Don't protect her by keeping her out," he shares. "That's not love. That's fear. You bring her in."

He's right. I know he's right.

Zack claps me on the back and says, "You'll figure it out. Blair is smarter than the average bear... like, she could have told you that you were an idiot, but instead she told you she needed space."

I nod, because he's right. Again.

"By the way, any news on her gym reopening?"

Leaning back, I squirt some water in my mouth—feeling that the break is almost over—and then say, "Her brother told me Thursday. Two days."

"Anything on that slime ball, Oscar? Benny is pissed."

I shake my head. "Nothing that everyone doesn't already know. Cops have kept it pretty quiet when it comes to details."

"To think, he thought he was speaking for us when he was in Dylan's office. Fucking dick. He'd hate to know how much support she actually has behind her. How cool we think she is for doing what she's doing. We'd fucking show up for her, that's for damn sure," he grumbles.

And, just like that, I have an idea.

We'd fucking show up for her. Of course we would.

Zack is walking back toward the field as I run up behind him, grabbing his shoulders. "I don't want your head to get much bigger than it already is, considering we're running out of extra-large helmets, but you sort of gave me an idea. And, hate to say it, but I definitely need your help."

"Only if you say please. And that I'm the best dressed player on the team." He raises his brows, never able to take much of anything seriously.

This fucking guy. "Please help me and yes, you're the best dressed player on the team."

He reaches an arm around my shoulder, shaking me, and asks, "What do you need?"

I start telling him my idea and his eyes light up. He's scheming and planning by the time we line up for more drills.

Not trying to get yelled at by Coach again, I do my best to pay attention.

But really, I'm reminding myself about how important it is to put yourself out there to get what you want.

Thirty-Eight

Blair

I'M ABOUT A MILE away and my knuckles are white as I grip the steering wheel. Today is the day I'm headed back to the studio. After the vandalism and my blow up with Tyson, I basically hid. My body needed a few days to get back to myself and feel like everything wasn't totally in despair—just a little.

I talked to the contractor and apparently the fixes went well. A new window, door, coat of paint, and fresh new security system, all of which was no big deal and completely covered by insurance. This time, I made sure to get cameras with the new system, kind of kicking myself for saying no to them before.

My heart tugs at the relief I thought I'd feel, knowing it wouldn't cost me anything financially, but then I remember what it took from me emotionally—it's a much higher price tag. Isn't that how it always goes?

I park in the back, on purpose, needing a moment alone. Running my thumb along the steering wheel, I go back to last week, including the game I missed. The points I didn't kick. The moment I didn't get to be part of. The anxiety that kept me on the edge of a breakdown.

At first, I was convinced I'd ruined it—let my team down, embarrassed myself by sitting out. But the coaches were incredible. My teammates checked in nonstop. Zack even left me a voicemail that made me laugh through tears, to accompany a massive basket full of every snack you could ever dream of.

Still, I hated how small I felt. How fragile everything was—the actual windows of the building a perfect metaphor for my resolve. How easily someone like Oscar could shake my foundation.

But even now, with the building back to its true form, there's still one crack I can't patch over.

Tyson.

I haven't talked to him since I found out about the house. *His* house. On his land. Michigan. States away. A future I was left in the dark on. It's hard not to overthink it.

I close my eyes for a second and the ache of not talking to him tugs somewhere deep in my chest. I miss him. Of course I miss him. I don't think there's ever been a time we've gone a whole week without saying something—some dumb joke, some late-night text.

And still, there's a sting I can't shake. Not from distance, exactly, but from the secret he kept. It shouldn't matter this much, but it does. If he's making plans somewhere else, away from me, what does that mean for us? He talked about the future, and I believed him. I still do, mostly.

It's a small crack, but it still hurts.

Before I get out of the car, I shake my hands out, trying to pull myself together. The gym is empty—I'd asked the staff to give me this first day alone. We're not open for members or anything; it's just me, trying to find my footing again. To stand inside the walls that hold so many good memories, and remember those instead of the ones who tried to take something that wasn't theirs.

The air whips against my cheeks as I wrap my scarf tighter and make the short walk to the back door. I punch in the new security code, step inside, and flip on the first lights.

I take a few steps in and turn the rest of the lights on, just as I feel someone standing in front of me. "Blair, I don't want to scare you," someone says and I immediately scream. And then I see that it's Dylan, and I stop.

My hand clutches my chest and my eyes feel like they might fall straight out of my skull. I yell, "What are you doing in here? What the fuck, Dylan?"

He steps back and says, "I'm so sorry. I didn't know the best way to not scare you. Tiffany, she let me in. I promise I mean no harm." When he steps forward, I steps back, needing to keep the space between us.

My breathing is shallow and quick, the air thin like there's none for me to grab. "What the hell are you doing in here?"

Dylan is trying not to smile as he says, "I'm sorry. We didn't really think this part through." He's trying not to laugh.

"We? What do you mean we?" When it's clear I'm not going to have a heart attack or pass out, I set my bag down on the floor, take my coat off and hang it on the hook.

My coach smiles at me, and nothing makes any sense. "Let me show you." He stands next to me, wrapping a cautious arm around my shoulder. We walk toward the main part of the gym and when we turn the corner, that's when I see them.

My teammates. Maybe the whole team. It's an entire room full of men, trying to be quiet and they're all wearing the same jersey.

My jersey. Around the room are balloons and a few 'Congratulations' banners hang from the ceiling across the mirrors.

When they see me, in unison, they yell, "Surprise!"

It makes me jump and, again, a heart attack isn't out of the question. When I can catch my breath, I ask, "What's all this?"

And that's when I see him. Tyson. Walking forward from the group, wearing the grin I dream about. A number seven on his front—he really is wearing my jersey.

"We wanted to try and show you how much we care. What happened with Oscar at the facility and then here, in the place you've built, wasn't okay. Actually, it was pretty fucked up."

Our teammates laugh from behind him at the brash honesty of his words. I catch myself almost smiling, the closest I've been in a week.

"Blair, we're some of your biggest fans. You deserved a welcome back that proved that to you." He says each letter of the word slow, on purpose, and it's an inside thing only the two of us know. How I told him to prove it to me—that he wanted more. "That you belong on the team, in Cosmos blue."

The guys immediately start to clap as Tyson finishes and before anyone else can say anything, I hear Zack yell from the corner, "WE LOVE YOU, BLAIR! THANKS FOR SAVING OUR ASS THIS SEASON."

Everyone claps and cheers for Zack. Cheers for me.

Coach Dylan steps in and says, "I'm so sorry for how that all happened. I should have called security the first time he crossed the line, and that's on me. I hope you're ready to come back to the team, to the facility, but if you're not—we get it."

The men around me all nod in understanding. They do get it. It might be true that they actually get me.

"Now, we have a photographer here, and we'd like to take some pictures that the Cosmos PR team can post—with your approval, of course—showing losers like whoever did this that we stand with you and you're part of our team. And *we're* the lucky ones."

A team photographer waves and starts putting us all together. I move where I'm supposed to as team members smile at me, give me high-fives, tell me good job. The entire time I'm trying not to melt into a puddle on the floor.

We take a few normal photos and then the guys ask if they can lift me on their shoulders. I let them do what they want, laughing the entire time. And I love the way the gym feels. Full. Brave. Safe.

"That's a wrap for us," Coach Dylan announces as he checks with the photographer that they got the shot. "We know you're getting back in the swing of things, but we hope to see you at practice tomorrow."

"You will. I promise." My voice comes out steadier than I feel.

Coach steps in close to me, looking between Tyson and myself. "And this? Nothing public until the season is over, okay? The rest of the team can be discreet if you can."

"You got it, Coach," I agree, my voice a little shaky.

The guys start to scatter—grabbing keys, slinging bags over their shoulders, still laughing about something Zack said. And one by one, they walk past me. Every single one of them is wearing my name on their back. My number.

It hits me harder than I expected.

For a second, I can't move. My throat burns, and I have to blink fast because it's suddenly too much—the sound of their voices, the sight of my jersey stretched across their broad shoulders, the way they showed up for me without being asked.

They didn't have to do this. None of them did. But they did. For me.

After this mess, they still chose to stand with me. To remind me that I mattered. That I was worth showing up for. I press a hand against my chest, right where the ache has lived all week, and it feels a little lighter now. Maybe this is what healing actually looks like—not a big, dramatic moment, just a quiet one where you realize you're not alone anymore.

I lock the back door behind them and walk back out to the person who I think is responsible for such a thing. Tyson.

When it's just the two of us, I can't help but practically run into his arms, letting him wrap me up. No matter what happens between us, I need him like this, right now. We hold onto each other, without saying anything, for who knows how long.

Tyson breaks the silence. "Come over here," he says, and he takes me to my own office. On my expo board are all the floor plans I saw at his place.

"This wasn't supposed to be a secret. But, I can see how it feels like I left you out. The thing is, I want you to help me build this house. I can't do it without you."

"You can't?"

"No. Why would I build our forever home without your opinion?" His eyes sparkle at the mention of forever.

Scrunching my eyes, I admit, "I'm barely following."

Tyson laughs and kisses me, slow and sweet. When he pulls away, he says, "Sorry, I've been waiting to do that." And he's wearing that devilish grin. "Back to this," he gestures to the board, "I bought this land years ago, not knowing what I wanted to do with it. I'd like to build a house there and I'd like it to be ours. You and me. Whether it's our main address or a vacation home, or even just our Thanksgiving home. I want to do this with you." His voice is sugary-sweet, dripping like honey off the side of the jar.

Ours.

"These plans were just ideas. Me taking a single meeting with a contractor who had a last minute cancellation on his books. I wanted to show them to you and get your non-negotiables and figure out what you had planned. What kind of things you need for your own version of forever."

My lip wobbles and my eyes are glassy, butterflies zooming around my rib cage as he adds, "Because, Blair, all I need is you. Michigan. New York. Anywhere else. It doesn't matter. My forever, my future, it's you."

I practically fall into his arms. He pulls me in tight, kissing my cheek before our lips find each other. My hands find the sides of his face and I hold him like I have no intentions of letting go.

"What do you say, baby? Want to help me build our house?" His nose brushes mine and his smile is contagious.

"Yes. A thousand times yes."

My lips find Ty's and I kiss him like it's the start of everything. The start of the two of us planning together. The start of our forever.

"I will never leave you, Blair. I promise. I'm staying right here, or wherever you end up."

"I know you will. And that's why I love you."

"And no more running from either of us. No more space. Let's work on it together." His voice may be soft but the man in front of me is the support I need.

No more running.

Fuck, I'm tired of running.

"For you, anything," I say. And I mean it. Because I know that the only running I want to do with Tyson is toward him. Toward us. Toward whatever is next.

Tyson picks me up, spinning me around, and I see my name on his back in the mirror. It heals a little bit of me, maybe the singed part where I was worried people will always leave. Because I'm finding out that's not necessarily true.

Sometimes, people will leave. Those that were never meant to stay and some who surprise you with their absence. The thing about people leaving, not choosing you, is that it gets you ready for what's coming. The people who stay. The ones who choose you, day after day, with blind confidence. People like Tyson.

Sometimes, people will show up when you least expect them. They'll cheer you on when you think you don't deserve it, pick you up when you can't do it on your own. And these are the people who are truly meant for us.

Tyson continues to spin me, and for once, I stop bracing for the drop. Because maybe I was never too much. Maybe I was just waiting for someone, the right person, who could hold it all.

Thirty-Nine

Tyson

I'M STILL WEARING BLAIR'S jersey as she wraps up the work she actually needed to do at Embers & Ashes. I can't help but smile at my reflection as I walk through the space, boasting so many mirrors to show me in my girl's jersey.

I'm so damn proud of her.

In order to pull this whole thing off, the team showing up for Blair, I had to come clean about what some may have wondered. I'm in love with her. How it started before she joined the team. How neither of us would ever let our relationship jeopardize anything remotely close to the Cosmos' success. I was rambling until one of my teammates stopped me, telling me they didn't care about that, and just to get to what they needed from me. What Blair needed. Even the coaching staff—they were all in.

That's all it took. I just had to ask. Everyone gave me a resounding *yes* and I'd be lying if I wasn't relishing in that feeling even after they left. The guys showing up for her and the way Blair reacted.

That smile. Like she was being seen. Even though I've been watching her for a decade.

And the stupid part—the part I can finally admit, with my whole fucking chest—is how much time I spent keeping that to myself. Like if I held everything inside, then no one could take anything from me.

I thought I was protecting us. But all I was doing was freezing myself out of my own life.

Because the second I stood toe to toe with the truth, with the woman of my dreams? It's been everything.

Not harder. Not even all that complicated. Just hopeful.

I drift through Embers & Ashes, the space somehow even more hers now after the work has been done to eradicate the vandalism. The team's energy still lingers in the air, laughter echoing faintly from where they helped surprise her earlier. Her jersey hangs warm on my shoulders, and every mirror reflects that fact back at me: I am hers. She is mine. We're done pretending otherwise.

I don't even realize where I'm going until I'm standing in front of the wall.

It takes up nearly the whole length of the back corner—strands of twinkling lights frame rows of Polaroid-style photos clipped up with tiny pink and black clothespins. Some are new from the last few months, others are older based on the dates written in permanent marker.

In every shot, someone stands smiling, flushed from a workout, holding a handwritten sign. *Hit my first 200-lb deadlift. Ran a mile without stopping. 100 spin classes.*

The wall has me smiling big enough that my cheeks fucking hurt. It's accomplishment after accomplishment, all possible and strung together by a common thread: Blair.

I stand there taking it in. She didn't just build a gym or a business—she built a place where people felt brave enough to try. Brave enough to not give up.

She showed up fully, honestly—every day. And look at what she created. Look at who she made people believe they could become.

My throat is tight as I look at all the photos, silently cheering them all on. I don't know if she actually realizes the way she's changing the world she lives in. It's not only what she's done for the members of Embers & Ashes, but showing up as the first woman in the NFL and not giving a fucking inch.

She's one of a kind. Unfucking real. And I hope I get to spend the rest of my life helping her realize.

"Hey." Her voice is soft and steady behind me. I turn and her eyes catch mine, like she's been watching me longer than I knew.

She looks at the wall, then back at me. "How long have you been standing here?" she asks, grinning but curious.

"Long enough," I say. My voice is rough, honest in a way it hasn't always been. "Long enough to realize I don't want to keep anything from the people who matter ever again."

Her expression softens, something warm blooming behind her eyes. "You ready to go?" she asks.

I take a breath, letting the truth settle into my bones.

"Yeah," I answer, stepping toward her, putting a soft kiss to her lips. "I'm ready."

Forty

Blair

My skin is hot being this close to Tyson without him touching me. The love of my life. The man I have no intention of living without.

Take-out containers have been long emptied and we've just been hanging out in my apartment. Just the two of us. I called Coach and confirmed I'd be at practice and anything else they needed me for this season.

I also shared, very clearly, that while this is one of the best things that's ever happened to me, it's a one-and-done sort of deal. I don't want to continue this, being on an active roster next season. Even if they wanted to find someone more experienced for the playoffs, I'd completely understand. Coach couldn't have been more gracious. He shared that they plan to use me, for as long as they can, to help the Cosmos win that next championship.

This has been incredible. Challenging in ways I'd never thought, including the hate and incident with Embers & Ashes. But even then, I don't know if I'd change it. The Cosmos have changed my life.

I may have made history, but this opportunity has changed my trajectory. It's because of my time with the Cosmos that I have interest and buy-in for the new Embers & Ashes locations... that's right, *multiple*.

My resilience has been tested in ways I never could've guessed and I'm proud of how I've come out on the other side. Well, there's still work to be done, and therapy appointments to attend, but this has helped me grow into a stronger leader. A stronger woman. An even more unstoppable force. And there's no way I'm running from that.

Plus, it brought me Tyson in a way I didn't know if I'd ever have him. Maybe the dominoes of fate would have fallen, just right, for us to take the leap outside of the friendzone without us being on the same team, but I guess we'll never know.

And you know what? I don't even care. There's no use worrying about what could've been, because I've got all I need, right here.

I must be staring because he smiles at me, waving a hand.

"Earth to Blair. What's going on in that head of yours?" His eyes practically sparkle when they look at me.

"Just thinking about you." I bite my lip. He's still in my jersey. His biceps pushing against the sleeves.

Fuck. It's hot.

"Oh, is that so? What about me?" he teases, and each syllable has the knots in my stomach pulling tighter.

I exhale. "Thinking about you in my jersey. How good you look."

The air sparks with tension and heat between us. Threads pull me closer to him, needing more.

"Definitely don't look better than you, baby." His words land and I'm in front of him a second later. I stand in front of him as he sits on the sofa. Slowly, I straddle him, one knee on each side of his thighs.

First, his mouth finds my neck and he kisses and licks up until he finds my mouth. His hands graze my hips until they land on my ass. I moan from his touch and he kisses me harder, like he's stealing all those sounds for himself.

My fingers dive into his hair, pulling on his brown locks, and that's all it takes for him to stand, holding me to him, then rearranging so he's carrying me with one arm under the bend of my knees and the other around my back.

He carries me like it's nothing and I fucking love it. My strong, professional football playing, athletic boyfriend. Lifting and easily carrying me to my bedroom.

Tyson tosses me on the bed and I let out a huff of breath and a laugh. When I see his erection pressing into his shorts, I know I'm going to be soaking for him in a matter of seconds.

Glancing down to his hard length, and then to me, he pushes his teeth over his bottom lip.

"You are in control, Blair. Need you to tell me what you want." His voice is stern and dances over every inch of me.

I hold back for a second, not knowing what to say. I sit up, going to reach for his shorts, and he literally takes a step back.

Ty's lip pulls up at the corners as he slowly shakes his head. "What do you want? What do we do next?"

I can tell by the look on his face that he's not going to give this up. I think about him wearing my jersey–showing me off–and how I want to see that.

Slowly, I gulp past the self-doubt trying to creep up. "I want you to fuck me from behind. Keep the jersey on. And I want to watch." The words are quicker than I'd hope, but he doesn't seem to notice. I tip my head to the mirror in the corner of my room.

Tyson says nothing as he walks across the space, picking up the mirror and situating it across the bed.

I'm taking off my clothes and feel like a sparkler that's about to go off. It's only been a few days since we've been together like this and it's making me all needy.

He takes his shorts down, his cock springing free and I'm lightly touching myself–my fingers circling my clit, just how I like it.

Tyson grabs my legs, pulls me down towards the edge of the bed. His hands are on my hips, flipping me to my belly before I can even register what's going on.

Next, I feel his lips kissing up the back of my legs. One and then the other—slow, meticulous, and like fucking torture I've *asked* to.

His fingers dig into my ass and his thumbs get close to my entrance. Fuck, I want him to touch me. Fuck me.

"What next, Blair?" His voice is bright and teasing.

I know if I'm not vocal, he'll wait until I give in. Tyson loves when I'm the one calling the shots, telling him what to do. I'm getting used to it.

"Eat me," I beg.

His tongue is lapping at me before I even get the words out. His hands find the front of my hips and he pulls me back onto my knees, so I'm on all fours as he licks me from behind.

Looking at the mirror, seeing us like this is almost enough to have me coming. The color of the jersey peeks out from behind me.

"Good boy," I praise the man who would literally do anything I asked.

He has me moaning, gripping the comforter with my hands. I try to move away from the pleasure but Tyson keeps me right where he wants me. Doing exactly what I asked for.

Each touch of his tongue, his fingers, his mouth, has me inching closer and closer to my orgasm. I don't want to come without him fucking me, so I tell him that.

"Okay, it's time. Fuck me in my jersey. I want to watch." I press myself up on my hands. I watch in the mirror as he stands, stroking his dick before pulling me closer to him.

He nudges at my entrance and he already knows I'm a puddle waiting for him. Slowly, he fills me. Moving in and out. A little further each time. And then he's hitting that sweet spot, the one that tells me I have all of him.

Tyson grips my hips and thrusts into me, faster, and I keep my eyes on the mirror. He's watching me as I watch him. He bites his lip as he fucks me and it's an incredible sight. My number. My jersey. On his front. I know my last name is on the back.

I'm afraid to blink, not wanting to miss any of it.

"Harder," I plead, my voice like gravel.

Tyson needs no other instruction as he tilts my hips just enough and pounds me mercilessly from behind. It's hard to breathe. And it's this almost painful type of euphoric bliss. Like, I need all of him, and when he pulls out, I'm craving him—stretching me to my max.

Tossing my hair out of my eyes, I focus on the image of him owning me from behind as my orgasm starts ripping through me, a cell at a time.

I can't keep my eyes open any longer and let out a scream as the waves try to pull me into another dimension. Only a few more pumps and Tyson comes inside me, filling me with his release.

He's relentless and a second orgasm is within my reach. The feeling of him inside me like this is something I've never experienced before... like one orgasm is finished, or so you thought, because here come the aftershocks. The muscles are so tight.

He doesn't stop until I'm trying to crawl towards the end of the bed. I can tell from his face that he's spent but he'll never stop until he knows I rode every wave.

I turn and lay on my back. Every nerve is raw. Exhaustion and bliss seep from my bones. His mouth is on mine and my arms loop around him.

I pull at him, needing his weight on me.

Ty knows what I need and is on top of me, still kissing me.

"That was..." I can't even find words.

All I can manage is looking at him, his eyes sparkling like sapphires and I feel the thread tightening around us, continuing to pull.

"I love you, Blair. Today. Now. Before. Every day." He's breathless and his words are quiet, but honest and true.

"I know, Ty. I love you too." And I kiss him, trying to say all the things that words could never even come close to.

Forty-One

Tyson

I HAVE A TEASPOON full of sprinkles I'm trying to shake just right for the whipped cream topping. Blair is sitting in her pajamas, which match mine, patiently waiting for her Christmas morning coffee.

It's been a few weeks since everything happened at Embers and Ashes. You can't tell anything was vandalized, well, except maybe the length of the waitlist to try and get gym time. Ever since the details have come out about Oscar and his treatment of Blair at the facility, support for her gym locations has vaulted into something more than a frenzy.

Some of our staff members have some loose lips—and I'm fucking proud of them. The Cosmos organization said that anonymous comments were acceptable, which they collected and gave to the reporting news outlets. I know that Zack and Benny both have comments that made it to print—and while a few of us know who it came from, every single person in that organization backs Blair.

Her memberships are sold out for a location that isn't even open yet. She's working on hiring staff to teach classes, because even if she can't be the one leading them, she wants to make sure they're done the Embers and Ashes way.

I'm in awe of her. Her determination. It seems like there are days where she has endless amounts of energy. Kicks her ass at a game or a training session and then is up late, doing anything she can fit in for Embers and Ashes' current and upcoming locations.

I'm so fucking proud of her.

We're a few weeks away from the post season and The Upstate Cosmos are at the top of our division. We've already earned the first week bye, which means a week of training while other teams fight for their championship dreams. Today, it's just the two of us celebrating our first holiday together. It seems odd to say, because Blair has always been right there, but this time it's different.

Tonight, my parents are flying in from Michigan, followed by Blair's mom and brothers. Tomorrow we'll do some brunch and city things while we celebrate the holiday together. We have a home game this week, so they'll stay for that, and head home after.

When I think about them all together in the seats we splurged on for part of their Christmas gift, it hits me like a punch to the gut. Everyone together, to see me and Blair play on the same field? A dream I didn't know I had.

"Ty, you're playing a dangerous game. Keeping my caffeine from me," her voice, cheerful and bright, says.

I smile while I get the rest of the sprinkles on the whipped cream. We've been making a new coffee syrup from scratch every week and this was my pick. I carry the mugs into the living room, careful not to spill, mostly because Blair views that as a cardinal sin... wasting caffeine like that.

Her lips tug up, breaking into the most contagious smile. She claps her hands in excitement and squeals, "What do we have here?" I swear, she has legit heart eyes as I set the mug down in front of her.

"Sugar cookie latte. Seemed perfect for today."

Her hands wrap around the mug, and she breathes it in. "Oh, that smells like heaven. In a cup."

"Heaven would be a coffee beverage for you. And cookies," I laugh as I sit next to her.

She turns to me. "And you."

I press a kiss to her lips. She smiles into it, and the space between us folds in on itself until there's nothing left but her. Honestly? It's making me fall even more in love with her. I didn't know if it was possible to feel more than I did when I had this massive, scary, hidden love for my best friend.

I was wrong. This is better. Much better.

Loving her was always this piece of me, bigger than I ever wanted to admit. And it took risking it all to find out what I was missing. But her loving me back is like my life clicking into place. Us together? More than I ever could've dreamt for.

She takes a sip of the coffee, her eyes dramatically rolling back into her head. "Tyson. This is the new number one. It's delicious."

I taste the latte and she's not wrong. It is a strong contender for our best one yet. "You say that every time we try a new one."

Blair shrugs her shoulders, taking another long drink of the coffee before setting it on the table to the side of the sofa.

I follow suit and then roll out the blueprints sitting in front of us. I've been so excited to get these in front of Blair—especially after we figured out that the land was completely buildable.

Ever since our fight, I made a promise to myself, and to her, that I wouldn't keep anything like this from her. Not again. I also made it a point to own up to Teague and let him know that his advice was *not* it. All jokes aside, I'm a grown man, and the accountability is mine to own. But it's fun to poke at your big brother when he's wrong.

This is the first time Blair and I will look at the blueprints after she told me about the house of her dreams. It wasn't much different than I envisioned, and everything she brought up fit right in with what I thought this house would be.

For now, we're calling it the Michigan house. We've not made any decisions on when or how it comes into play. Hell, maybe we'll only stay there when we're celebrating holidays or for vacations. There's more than enough time to figure that out. I plan to spend the rest of my life with Blair, wherever she takes me.

I walk her through the blueprints, showing her all the rooms. I pause, trying to let her take it in.

"This one is new?" She points to a square on the blueprint.

She's right.

"That is your office. I want you to have a place that's completely your own. It can be a surprise when I see it for the first time. All your own space."

"You don't have to do that."

"At the rate you're creating an Embers and Ashes empire? You need it. And it's not about having to do it—I want to."

She grabs the front of my shirt and pulls me to her. Our noses touch when she says, "Thank you for loving me, Ty."

"You make it easy, baby," I say back to her before putting my mouth to hers. Kissing her for all the times I felt like I couldn't or was too afraid to cross the line.

I have a lot to make up for—loving someone secretly for a decade will do that—but you know what? That's a challenge I'm more than willing to accept.

Blair? She's more than worth it. The type of woman who you get a hold of, you do everything in your power, and maybe then some, to let go. Loving her is a privilege.

And I'm the luckiest man in the world.

The Game Day Tribune

COSMOS FALL SHORT OF SUPER BOWL, BUT HAVE THEY ALREADY WON?

UPSTATE, N.Y. – The Upstate Cosmos came within three yards of punching their ticket to another Super Bowl appearance on Sunday night. But in a heartbreaking turn of events, a last-second fumble on the three-yard line–recovered and returned for a touchdown by the Bulldogs–sealed their fate and ended the Cosmos' season.

To call it a fumble might be generous to the defense; the ball was punched out with precision by a relentless Bulldogs defense. Even the league's top running back couldn't withstand the punishing pressure in those final moments.

Yet, amid the heartbreak, one storyline continues to rise above the loss: Blair Miller.

Since Week 5, the Cosmos' rookie kicker has been nothing short of remarkable. On Sunday, she was perfect–nailing all four extra-point attempts and drilling a 22-yard field goal. Each time Miller took the field, the energy inside the stadium shifted. Fans knew they were witnessing something historic.

The Game Day Tribune

Typically, postgame chatter focuses on what went wrong—the missed opportunities, the turnovers, the "what ifs." But this Monday, that conversation feels misplaced. The Cosmos' season deserves more than scrutiny; it deserves celebration.

This is a team that took a chance early in the year on a young woman with undeniable talent and composure. That decision not only reshaped their season—it helped redefine the sport itself. Around upstate New York and beyond, fans wearing jerseys emblazoned with Miller on the back stood and cheered, honoring the player who changed what was possible in the NFL.

Blair Miller has been more than a standout rookie; she's been a symbol of progress. While some critics may remain skeptical, their doubts only add fuel to a growing movement toward inclusion and innovation within the game.

Whether or not the Cosmos made it to the Super Bowl, Miller's contribution has made us all feel like winners today.

Blair Miller—thank you.

Forty-Two

Blair

"I CAN'T BELIEVE YOU own so much pink," Tyson says to Zack, who is wearing an almost-neon blazer with matching loafers.

Grinning like it's his job, he counters, "If you must know, this was my Super Bowl pre-game fit. We obviously aren't playing, so I had to at least wear it tonight." He swipes at an invisible piece of lint on his shoulder.

My heart sings as Tyson and Zack banter back and forth. When we lost in the conference final, I didn't know what this night would look like for them. I was bummed—I would have loved to have had an opportunity to play for a championship—but those feelings of missing out weren't the same compared to the guys.

I'm not sure what I was expecting, but they handled the loss a hundred times better than whatever I was hoping for. Sure, everyone was disappointed, but they kept it together until we made it back to the locker room. There were tears. Hugs. Teammates being proud of each other—some in the last year of their contract and not knowing what comes next.

It was clear from the team's reaction and the coaching staff's closing remarks: we had a hell of a season and had nothing to be sorry about.

Zack has decided to host a party tonight, inviting his closest teammates and their families to watch the game. I can't wait for my brother to show up; it's going to be so much fun.

For now, we're the first ones here, arriving early like Zack requested. He needed Tyson's help hanging up some décor—which turned out to be almost life-size cutouts of the teammates he invited. Each one has our name, number, position, and a fun fact that Zack gleaned from us throughout the season.

Tyson's fun fact reads "Knows The Greatest Showman soundtrack by heart," and mine is "The queen of ordering the perfect amount for the table at any restaurant."

"Blair! Finally!" someone yells, and I turn to see the most gorgeous crimson curls I've ever seen on someone. Emilie. Zack's wife.

She practically runs over and then opens her arms for a hug. "I'm Emilie! It's so good to finally meet you. Blair Miller... in person!"

I lean in and let her hug me. "Thank you for having us. Everyone is so excited. And I screamed when Zack told me you'd be here," I gush, cheeks pinching from smiling.

"Here I am." She spins and it's official: I'm obsessed with her. The sound of glass breaking pulls her attention from me to wherever Zack is causing some chaos. She rolls her eyes but doesn't look annoyed in the slightest. "I have to check on that, but you and me... later. Okay? I want to know everything." She squeezes my shoulder as she heads to wherever Zack is sweeping up glass shards.

When it's just the two of us, Tyson waves me over to the patio.

Snow drifts and sparkles through the February night as the sun starts to go down. The outdoor space has fire tables and containers of steamy cocktails—wouldn't expect anything less from the host that is Zack Andersen.

Tyson grabs a mug and fills it with a 'boozy even though we loozy' hot chocolate. We both laugh at the name, and I make a mental note to tell Zack that it made us *actually* laugh. Tyson takes a spot on a loveseat, blankets and pillows strewn about, and I sit next to him. He immediately wraps a blanket around our shoulders.

I take a sip of my hot chocolate—definitely boozy and absolutely delicious—and lean into Tyson.

"Do you remember the last time we were out here?" he asks, taking a sip of his own hot cocoa.

I nod, grinning. "Yes. Halloween. Could never forget." I bump my shoulder into his.

His eyes turn to me, blue and bright. "I wanted to kiss you so bad. And then someone came out here yelling about coffee beans." Tyson laughs—the kind that warms my belly.

He's right. It was the closest almost—the moment we were about to cross. "The most epic I-think-you're-going-to-kiss-me-but-you-never-do moment," I say, almost mocking myself as I go back to the phrase.

As soon as the words are out of my mouth, Tyson's lips are on mine. The kiss is sweet and full, like a promise we're both eager to keep.

When he pulls back, his forehead presses to mine as he murmurs, "I'm always going to kiss you, Blair Miller. Every chance I get."

"I know you will," I reply before pressing my lips back to his.

I've never trusted anything the way I trust us. Tyson lifts me up, challenges me, and somehow always makes the world feel steadier beneath my feet. I'm desperate—in the best way—to see what's next for us.

Because wherever that is, whatever comes our way, we'll choose each other. We'll fight for this love in every city, every season, and every adventure.

It's time to be all in. Together. No more loving each other from the sidelines.

THE END

WANT A LITTLE MORE BLAIR AND TYSON? SCAN THE QR CODE FOR THE BONUS CONTENT!

Did you know both Tripp and Zack
each have their own books?
Read all about them in...

YOUR PLAY TO CALL

&

YOUR RULE BREAK

What's next for
Rachel LaBerge

Scan for upcoming preorders!

ACKNOWLEDGMENTS

I'm so thankful to have been included in a project like this. I'll never forget what it was like to get this invite, the opportunity to contribute to a series all about strong women in sports. I couldn't say yes fast enough.

The idea of Blair and Tyson was kind of bopping around my brain ever since I wrote YOUR SECRET TO KEEP but that series felt truly finished to me, so, this new book gave me the chance to give these two the home they deserved.

To one of my favorite group chats, 'girls who podcast'... Carly and Mollie. I legit couldn't have done this without you. The way you both cheered me on to get to the finish line is something I'm so thankful for. XOXO.

To my alpha and beta readers... COULDN'T HAVE DONE THIS WITHOUT YOU! From the swooning and screaming over your favorite parts and the questions you asked to help me get to the magic of their story, I am so grateful. Thanks for always taking a chance on me.

To Kendra, my editor and friend, thank you. You make me feel like this is a club I belong to and couldn't do this without someone like you. Thank you for all you do to support me, my work, and my bad habit of shifting tenses.

To my readers, the person who is holding on to this right now, thank you for making my dream come true. I love telling stories and can only do this because you give my books and my ideas a chance. It means more than I can try to explain.

To Robby, my green-flag husband, thanks for giving me the space to do things like this. This includes watching me yell at a TV, like players can hear me, more often than I'd care to admit. I love you.

ABOUT THE AUTHOR
Rachel LaBerge

Rachel LaBerge is best known for writing love stories where the characters' brains are spicy, just like the plot...

When she's not reading or writing, she's probably watching a sporting event, thinking about donuts, sour candy, or looking for her next hyperfixation. She lives in Michigan with her husband (Roberto), her two Frenchies (Rafa and Ruby), and cat (Riley).

You can connect with her on Instagram, TikTok, and Threads @rachellabergeauthor (no 'R' name required).